BIRTHDAY SHOT

A LOVE ON THE ROCK BOOK

RILZY ADAMS

Copyright © 2020 by Rilys "Rilzy" Adams

All rights reserved.

No part of this book may be reproduced in any form or by any electronic or mechanical means, including information storage and retrieval systems, without written permission from the author, except for the use of brief quotations in a book review.

To everyone who has taken a chance on my work.

CHAPTER ONE

Shae Abbott moved her hips in her office chair as she sang along to KES The Band's 'Wotless'. She wrapped up Trinidad's Carnival a few weeks before and was looking forward to heading to Jamaica to experience it all over again with the unique features a different island brought. The vibrant soca beats pumping through her headphones had her wishing she was parading along the Savannah in full costume, getting on just as 'Wotless' as the song proclaimed. Shae always tried to ensure her blog was varied in its content, but she looked forward to her Carnival posts the most. She'd be the happiest woman alive if she could spend her entire life roaming from one Carnival to the next. Her screensaver was steadily counting down the days to Jamaica's Carnival but it was more of a buzzkill than anything else. She had to get through two whole months before she could let loose on the streets of Kingston. She sighed and swallowed her anticipation with her now lukewarm iced coffee.

"This will have to do," she murmured as she perused Spotify for more of her favorite soca tunes. She turned up the volume on her laptop as she continued scrolling through the myriad of photos she'd taken during her time in Trinidad trying to figure out which would work seamlessly with the blog post she was curating. *Influencer*. Shae never thought in a million years that she'd make a living, and a good one too, from creating Internet content. When she was growing up these sorts of careers didn't even exist. Her father still couldn't pin down exactly what Shae did and just went about telling people she was "a big thing on the Internet" when they asked. She still chuckled whenever he told her that. She wasn't a *big thing* by any means, but with over a hundred and fifty thousand YouTube subscribers and nearly double that on Instagram, Shae wasn't doing too badly. Especially for a girl from a rock in the Caribbean Sea. She had just about selected her first round of photos when Beyonce's 'Flawless' started blaring. Shae rolled her eyes at the ringtone her best friend, Jada, had set for herself.

"Yes, my love?"

Jada chuckled. "You really need to stop sending passive aggressive messages to your ex."

Shae couldn't stop the mirth that flowed from her lips. Jada seemed to drop whatever she was doing whenever the notification for a new blog post popped up. Her best friend was always on the phone with her commentary within fifteen minutes of Shae pressing the publish button. She'd only published her last blog post ten minutes ago. The post focused on the dangers of trying to change to fit someone else's preference and how it never worked out in the end. It was great advice for her followers but Jada knew Shae spoke from very personal experience.

"I'm doing no such thing," she protested. She was doing exactly that, but she wasn't going to admit it.

"Wasn't I there for you enough?" Jada asked, her voice filled with teasing energy. "Did you need more ice-cream? More tequila? A therapist? Square ass Angus was too bland for you and you know it. Leave him to his rectangular ass Gertrude and stop shooting petty shots."

"His wife's name is Giselle."

"I said what I said," Jada responded. "I'm not arguing with you because the advice is pretty solid. But you need to *let it go*. Anyway, I'm off. See you at the party."

Jada disconnected the call before Shae could defend herself, but she guessed it was just as well because her friend probably wouldn't listen to anything she had to say. She and Angus dated during the tail end of her Human Resources degree at the University of the West Indies' Jamaican campus while he was finishing up his law practicing qualifications at the Norman Manley Law School. They were great together, she was in love and honestly believed he was her future. Shae chuckled, even now, when she remembered how silly she'd been. Angus became a lawyer and was quick to dump her on her ass because he thought her desire to try her hand at YouTube was an embarrassment. He had aspirations of being a judge and didn't think someone with such lack of direction was a good fit for him. Shae had taken the breakup hard, the blow to her confidence even harder and she was devastated when he started dating a coworker shortly after. The years had passed and Shae thought she put it all behind her but his recent marriage to that same coworker was bringing out the petty in her. She pushed the bitterness away and returned to the blog post she hoped to publish in the next few days. She had too many other things to concern herself with besides Angus. Her brother, Sheldon's, engagement party was that afternoon and she was helping her mother in the kitchen all day. Heat crept to her cheeks when she thought about who Sheldon's party would drag in. Yes, Shae decided, she had way more dangerous things to concern herself with.

CHAPTER TWO

Shae raised the tray of barbecued chicken wings she was carrying into the air, narrowly avoiding colliding with two of her baby cousins who were more concerned with their energetic game of *tag-a-man* than safety. Trevaughn's high-pitched, five-year-old squeal rang out as he zoomed around Shae, eager to avoid Kaiden catching up to him and touching him. One touch from Kaiden would render Trevaughn 'it' and he'd have to run around until he caught someone else. Shae laughed. She used to be extremely aggressive whenever she played that game with her cousins and friends. She still had a few scars to prove it. She made her way to the large, rectangular, plastic table tucked away in the corner of her parents' backyard. It was already filled with a bunch of finger food; salt-fish cakes, pumpkin and banana fritters, fried chicken, patties, sausage rolls and meatballs. There were two similar tables filled with alcohol because what proper West Indian party didn't have a disproportionate amount of liquor to food? The party was already going full swing when she stopped to survey the scene in front of her. There were a few groups of people sitting on the wooden picnic benches under the broad tamarind tree playing dominoes.

Other persons congregated in different sections of the large yard, chatting excitedly or dancing to the loud strains of the Burning Flames' song permeating the air alongside the tempting scents wafting from the barbecue grill her father manned.

"Your daddy going to burn the chicken if he don't stop dancing and pay attention."

Shae chuckled as she passed the tray to Jada, who'd agreed to help for the party. "You know that man looks for any excuse to pelt his waist."

"Where are the guests of honor, anyway?" Jada asked. She pulled her locs on top of her head into a messy topknot. "I didn't expect them to be late for their own engagement party."

Shae checked her watch. It was inching up to five PM and her older brother, Sheldon, and his fiancée, Kara, were still not there. The engagement party had a three PM starting time but everything was running on Antiguan time so things officially started nearly an hour late.

"They had to make an airport run," Shae said. "Kofi flew in for the engagement party."

She spoke quickly hoping Jada would be too busy sorting out the finger food table to pay much attention to what she said but she knew it had been too much to hope for as soon as her best friend looked up at her with a glint in her dark brown eyes. This was exactly why she conveniently forgot to tell Jada Kofi was coming.

"Kofi? Kofi Matthews, Kofi?" she asked.

Shae pursed her lips and rolled her eyes. "Really, Jae? How many Kofis do you know?"

"Two if you count fine ass Kofi Siriboe and I know his behind ain't coming to Sheldon's engagement party," her friend said with a huge grin that earned her a scowl from Shae.

"The flight was a little delayed," Shae continued, choosing

to ignore just how excited the new information made Jada. "They should be here soon."

She turned to head back to the kitchen to get the final trays of food when Jada grabbed her arm. "You wearing *that*?"

Shae glanced down at the olive green midi dress she'd grabbed from her closet with little thought earlier that afternoon. She raised an eyebrow. "What's wrong with it?"

"Come on," Jada fussed. "This is Kofi. Kofi Matthews, Kofi"

"Why do you keep saying his name like that?"

"You've had a crush on this guy since you were eleven!"

"Twelve. And it was a childhood crush," Shae said. "*Was*."

Jada narrowed her eyes. "Didn't you guys almost kiss a few years ago?"

Shae's face went hot. "Stop being dramatic, Jada. No, we didn't *almost kiss* a few years ago. I'm going back to the kitchen."

"Get me some popcorn while you're in there," Jada called after her. "Cause it will definitely get interesting once Kofi shows up."

Shae refused to look back at Jada even though her heart thumped against her chest. She wiped her palms on her dress, annoyed Jada got into her head. She *had* been a bit off kilter ever since her mother casually mentioned how sweet it was that Kofi decided to fly in for Sheldon's engagement party a few days before. But that had nothing to do with her still having feelings for him. She *couldn't* still have feelings for him. Shae kept up with Kofi on social media with the odd messages here and there but she hadn't seen him in person in years. That was more by design than anything else. Jada remembered that *almost kiss* more fondly than it was. What actually happened was Shae's tipsy, enamored ass thought Kofi was coming in for a kiss while saying goodbye to her after a party when he was just trying to give her a peck on the cheek. She still remembered the slightly amused look on his face and his soft voice going, *"Whoa. What are you doing?*" when he realized she was about to kiss him. It had been nearly four years and Shae still wanted to sink into the ground whenever she thought about it. She was still cringing at the memory as she bent over and started removing the mini quiches that had been browning in the oven.

"Shae Butter!"

She swore under her breath, desperately trying to keep the tray in her hands from falling. She wouldn't hear the end of it from her mother if she dropped the quiches all over the hardwood floor. Shae waited until the tray was safely on the island before she took a deep breath and turned to face the newcomer in the kitchen. Kofi was smiling with his arms extended as he walked towards her. She crashed against his chest when he pulled her into a tight hug. Shae gasped involuntarily. Kofi was a lot firmer than she remembered him being. His hair was about half an inch longer than the low cut he usually rocked, and he'd grown a thick, full beard. She'd seen the beard on social media, but she was unprepared for just how much she wanted to run her fingers through it. His yellow polo shirt accentuated his deep brown skin in ways that made it hard for Shae to tear her eyes away. Damn. The years had done Kofi so disgustingly well that it bordered on disrespectful.

"Hey Kofi," she finally said when she was able to stop herself from staring. "It's been a while."

His thick lips pulled back to reveal straight white teeth and deep dimples in each cheek. Shae had to remind herself to breathe.

"I started thinking maybe that was intentional," he said.

Shae's chuckle was filled with more nervous energy than she expected. "Intentional? Why would I be intentionally avoiding you?"

He smiled wider and those damn dimples deepened. Shae's stomach tightened and she knew she needed to make her escape. It was only when she tried to take a step back that she realized Kofi still had his hands around her waist. He started speaking but stopped when Sheldon strolled into the kitchen calling out for him. They both pulled away from each other so quickly that Shae almost knocked over the tray of quiches she'd been so careful to safeguard.

"Everything okay here?" Sheldon asked. His eyes darted from Shae to his best friend who was busy stealing a quiche from the tray. Shae smacked his hand. "Leave them alone."

He took a bite and Shae found it hard to pull her attention from the way his lips wrapped around the pastry, imagining those lips somewhere else entirely.

"I'll catch you around," he said. Shae was just starting to tune back into what was going on around her when both Sheldon and Kofi stalked off, leaving her standing in her mother's kitchen desperately clenching her thighs together.

"What was *that*?"

She spun around to find Kara leaning against the fridge with an amused smirk on her face. "How long have you had the hots for Kofi?"

"Lower your damn voice," Shae mumbled. "I don't need your nosey fiancé wandering in here."

Kara clapped her hand over her open mouth. "Lawd Jesus! You do!"

"I don't," Shae said. She met Kara's unconvinced hazel eyes and quickly amended her statement. "I liked him a little when I was a kid, but that's old, old news now."

Her soon to be sister-in-law shrugged. "Not from where I was standing."

CHAPTER THREE

Well, damn.

Little Shae Abbott had grown the entire fuck up. Kofi and Sheldon had been best friends since they were six years old after a challenge to see who could climb a mango tree fastest ended with Kofi fracturing his arm. He'd been in and out of the Abbott's home for his entire life, so he'd seen every embarrassing moment of Shae growing up. He remembered when she was that annoying little sister always underfoot and he and Sheldon did their best to avoid her. Then there were the awkward preteen and early teenage years when he always caught her staring when she thought he couldn't see. Sheldon wouldn't stop teasing her about her obvious crush on him. His best friend would corner his little sister singing, "Shae and Kofi sitting in a tree, k–i–s–s–i–n–g" until Shae would run out of the room unable to look at anyone. Sheldon might have found it funny but all Kofi felt was discomfort. He tried to handle the crush as delicately as he could. He was friendly enough to Shae in hopes she didn't feel as awkward as Sheldon seemed hellbent on making her feel. But he tried to maintain enough distance so she never thought he reciprocated her feelings. There were three years between him and Shae. It didn't seem like a lot at twenty-nine and thirty-two but it was massive when he was sixteen and she was thirteen. It still seemed like a huge difference when Shae turned seventeen and an almost twenty-year-old Kofi returned home from university during Christmas break and started noticing her for the first time. That he suddenly found her attractive made Kofi feel seven shades of fucked up. So, he learned to keep his distance. They were friendly enough that he teased her by calling her Shae Butter when she cut off her back length relaxed hair in favor of growing out her natural curls. Those natural curls now had golden streaks and were styled in a fluffy twist out that fell to her collarbone. Her cinnamon skin's dewy glow left him wanting to kiss it to see if she tasted of sunshine. He wondered, more than once, if her round, russet colored eyes would widen if he kissed her rosebud lips. Shae was already gorgeous as hell as a young woman, but now she was all grown. She'd filled out her grown woman body and Kofi's ached just looking at her. Her hips and thighs were thicker in the best way possible, her breasts fuller and *that ass*. Kofi had almost swallowed his tongue when he stepped into the kitchen and found her bent over the oven with the material of her dress clinging to her ass. His mind went wandering in directions it had no business going, and all of those directions included some variation of Shae's legs spread wide and his head buried between them.

"You okay?"

Sheldon's voice snapped him out of his thoughts. He could barely meet his best friend's eyes, knowing he'd just been imagining his little sister spread-eagle against their mother's island as he pleasured her with his mouth.

"A bit tired," he lied. "The flight was long."

Sheldon didn't need to know he'd slept nearly five out of the eight-hour flight from London to Antigua.

"I understand if you need to go," Sheldon said. Kofi knew he should take advantage of Sheldon's suggestion, but he assured his friend he was fine. He wanted to stick around to see if he could get Shae alone again. Kofi was about to get himself a drink when Sheldon asked, "What was happening between you and Shae in there?"

"What are you talking about?"

"You guys looked kind of cozy."

Kofi breathed out his annoyance. "I was hugging a friend I haven't seen in a long ass time. You really still on this bullshit?"

"I'm not *still* anything. That's my baby sister," Sheldon said, unfazed by how annoyed Kofi was.

"There's nothing babyish about Shae anymore, bruv," Kofi said and chuckled when Sheldon glared at him. Kofi could never point out when Sheldon stopped finding Shae's crush on him funny. Sheldon had never been an overprotective brother, but something seemed to change once Shae started growing up. He probably would've threatened every male off her if he could. But he couldn't. So he seemed to save his warnings for Kofi. *"You're my brother so she's your sister"* was one of his refrains and Kofi always only barely managed stop himself from pointing out that Shae was definitely not his sister. Sheldon had made his views clear. And then kept making them clear over and over again. Kofi quickly decided curiosity wasn't a good enough reason to ruin his closest friendship. He'd come close once, though. He'd had a bit too much alcohol and Shae looked a little too good in that short, shimmery gold dress she'd worn to a New Year's Eve party. Sheldon and Kara had hightailed out of there long before the New Year and Kofi promised he'd see to it Shae got home safely. He'd been happy to. He and Shae had spent more time alone together during that trip home than they had for the entire time they'd known each other. Sheldon was in the new exciting phase of his relationship with Kara and was forever bailing on things they planned. Kofi was never quite sure if Shae had just taken pity on him or if any lingering remnants of her crush remained. It didn't matter. During the times they spent chatting on her family's couch, the two hikes with her friends she'd suggested he joined her on and the parties where they ended up in a corner dancing together, Kofi felt his interest in Shae spark. It was something deeper, more potent and dangerous than curiosity. But he'd pushed it away because he knew better than to allow himself to feel anything for Sheldon's little sister. Except, he hadn't been prepared for how affectionate Shae got when she was tipsy. When he'd dropped her home after the party, she'd wrapped her hands around his waist and leaned into him so that her soft breasts splayed against his chest. He'd already been struggling with control when she pulled back and fixed him with those big, brown eyes. He'd been halfway to kissing her adorable ass when he remembered Sheldon and played it off like he had been planning to give her a friendly kiss on the cheek. He didn't miss the mortification in Shae's eyes and he always suspected that their near kiss was the reason she'd become so damn scarce over the last few years. She was always quick to respond to messages on social media and the odd email he'd sometimes send her way but whenever he actually managed to return to Antigua, she always flaked on any suggested meet ups. She'd been in London less than a year before to take part in a natural hair expo and Kofi hadn't even been aware until she posted the vlog a few days after she'd left.

Kofi caught a glance of Shae wandering back out into the yard and being stopped by perverted Uncle Larry who'd been telling anyone who came within earshot that the secret to aging well was white rum and pussy. The eighty-year-old man said something and Shae threw her head back laughing. Kofi couldn't pull his eyes away from her. Nearly four years ago, he put Sheldon's feelings above his desire for his best friend's little sister. He thought back to how soft and pliant she felt against his body when he hugged her in the kitchen. Kofi wasn't sure he would, or could, make the same decision again.

CHAPTER FOUR

Thirty.

Shae interlocked her hands and stretched them above her head. *Thirfrigginty.* Her life was nothing like she'd expected it to be at this point, but it was even better in so many ways. She had a job she adored, a close-knit group of friends and an amazing family. She was happy. She was successful. She was fulfilled. Well, mostly fulfilled. Shae glanced at her watch and debated whether she had enough time to pull out the vibrator she kept in the drawer of her bedside table. Her cellphone started blaring Beyonce before she could decide. Shae laughed. She guessed Jada was up. Shae answered with her mouth still curved into a grin, knowing her best friend would be extra... as always. Jada launched into a boisterous rendition of 'Happy Birthday' that seemed to be the love child of the traditional and the Stevie Wonder version. It was just as out of tune as Shae expected it to be.

"How does it feel to be over the hill?" Jada teased.

"You know I can't stand you, right?"

But Shae was laughing.

"Are you excited about later?"

"Of course!" she admitted. "Ridiculously so."

Shae had gone through many ideas for her thirtieth birthday. She thought about taking a solo trip to Italy. Rome, Portofino and Naples were high on her travel bucket list and she knew they would provide excellent content for all of her social media platforms. She and Jada considered hitting up Vegas with two of their closest friends, Brianna and Raelynn. She knew that would make for a tipsy, action packed vacation and she filed it away as a trip she definitely wanted to take in the future. Shae eventually decided to celebrate her thirtieth with a massive, nostalgia-filled house party featuring only mid-90s to mid-2000s dancehall music. She liked the idea of being able to celebrate with a lot of her friends and she thought it would be a cool way to introduce her non-Caribbean followers to more of her culture. She convinced her parents to let her use their house since it was much larger than the one she rented. At first they were against it but finally caved when she offered to put them up at one of their favorite hotels and promised the house would be spotless when they returned.

"We will start getting things together as soon as your parents leave for their breakfast date with you."

"Are you sure you don't...."

Jada cut her off, just like Shae expected she would. "Me and Regina got this sorted. All you need to be concerned about is getting your fat ass in those *pum pum* shorts and finding somebody to dick you down right later."

"Jada!"

"Look," her best friend said. "We all know birthday sex doesn't count."

Shae chuckled. "Oh, really?"

"Yes, really. Find somebody and shoot your birthday shot," Jada said. "And we both know whose fine ass just flashed through your mind."

"I *really* can't stand you."

"Sure Shae, I totally believe that," Jada laughed. "Go get ready to have breakfast with your parental units. We'll resume this conversation later."

SHAE STARTED her birthday with her parents and Sheldon for as long as she could remember. When she was school aged, her mother would always make an extravagant spread for breakfast and occasionally allowed her to miss the first half of the school day. She looked forward to the tradition fiercely. It was definitely one reason she decided to stay in Antigua instead of traveling for her thirtieth, even if she hadn't realized it. They decided on a restaurant on the outskirts of St. John because Shae was obsessed with their cocktails, four cheese omelets and the ultra modern décor. She'd thrown on a blush pink dress with gold, chunky heels and gold accessories. Her hair was still in the two strand twists she'd put in the night before to prepare for the twist out she planned to wear for her birthday party. Her makeup was minimal, but Shae was very pleased with the result. She spent more time in her full-length mirror trying to get a good photo for her Instagram feed than she should have. Shae never expected to fall into an online career, and she didn't take the privileges that came with it for granted. If that meant she would be a little late for breakfast with her parents in order to get a few photos for her blog and Instagram feed, she'd gladly do it. She was thankful that the people closest to her understood. Well, almost all of them. Grace Abbott hated tardiness so Shae wasn't surprised her mother had already sent her two texts by the time she rushed into Simply Coffee fifteen minutes later. She'd planned to take some photos of the all white and cream furnishings with the pops of color and exposed faux-brick wall that accented the minimalist décor, but she figured it might be better to pull out her camera after she quelled her mother's annoyance. She was thinking of the best way to capture her birthday breakfast for her blog, *Island Gyal Tings,* as her eyes searched the restaurant for her family. All her thoughts crashed to a halt when she finally spotted them sitting in the corner of the restaurant closest to the seventy-inch flat screen TV that displayed the menu. She'd expected her mother, father, Sheldon and Kara, but she did not expect to see Kofi there, leaning in to say something to her smiling mother with his fingers wrapped around his cocktail. All eyes turned on her at the same time. Kofi's smile widened and Shae's stomach somersaulted. She forced her feet to move towards the table where she kissed her parents' cheek and sat in the only available seat between Kofi and Kara. She wished someone, *anyone,* had given her the heads up that Kofi would be there. And not just there. He was there looking so fucking amazing that she found it hard to breathe. His white T-Shirt stretched across his broad chest and revealed biceps she couldn't help but imagine flexing as he hovered over her during sex. She clenched her thighs together as she took a deep breath and chewed on her bottom lip. Kofi looked good as fuck but he smelled even better. The spicy, woodsy scent tickled her nose but it was the notes of orange and lemon that made her want to curl herself around him and inhale like some deranged kitten. Her stomach tightened. Jesus. This was going to be a long ass breakfast.

"I'm surprised to see you here," she said, trying to distract herself from her pussy's incessant throbbing. Kofi smirked and she swallowed nervously. Had she kept her voice as light and unaffected as she'd intended to?

"Sheldon invited me," Kofi said. "I hope you don't mind me crashing your birthday festivities." His deep, warm voice felt like fingertips brushing down her spine. Shae squeezed her eyes shut. She tried to find her voice but Sheldon started speaking before she could make her mouth move.

"Of course she doesn't mind," her brother said. He took a sip of his coffee before he continued, "You're a big brother to her."

Kara gave Sheldon a side eye before meeting Shae's gaze and smirking. "Sheldon," she said. "That man is *not* Shae's brother."

"Are you okay with me crashing your party too?" Kofi continued as if Sheldon hadn't spoken at all. He pulled his bottom lip through his teeth, smiling slowly and mischievously when he added, "Sis."

Shae almost forgot to breathe, but Kara's soft laughter pulled her out of it.

"You're always welcome." Shae cringed. Did her voice squeak? She was at the grand ass age of thirty, but somehow Kofi still turned her into a twelve-year-old.

"I'll remember that, Shae Butter"

His voice was low and flirty, but nobody else seemed to be paying them much mind. Shae wondered if she was imagining things but didn't have a lot of time to sit with her thoughts because a server popped up with a bright smile to take their orders. Shae found it hard to concentrate on the conversations going on around her with Kofi's leg pressed up against hers. He wore khaki shorts so their skin pressed together below the knees and Shae wanted to jump out of her skin.

"Is everything okay Care Bear?" her father asked. Shae was so off-kilter sitting next to Kofi feeling his body heat, inhaling his scent and aching for him that her father's nickname for didn't even embarrass her.

"I'm great," she said, forcing the widest, brightest smile she could. "Why?"

"You look a bit spaced out," her mother piped up. "Did you exert a lot of energy ringing your birthday in?"

Grace didn't even try to hide the innuendo in her voice.

Shae groaned as she flicked her eyes to Kofi to see him looking at her with open curiosity in his brown eyes. Her mother's teasing drew a sharp look from her father.

"She's thirty years old, Garvin," her mother said. "We'd been having sex for years by then."

"Mom!"

Kara and Kofi chuckled at the absolute horror in Shae and Sheldon's voice.

"I rang in my birthday fully rested," Shae said desperately wanting to put an end to the conversation. "I went to sleep at eight."

Shae only hoped to put her mother's teasing and father's discomfort to rest but immediately wished she hadn't spoken when Kofi squeezed her thigh and said, "Wise move, Shae Butter. You'll need your energy for tonight. Make sure you save me a dance."

"I might," Shae teased even though dancing was the furthest thing from her mind with the warm heaviness of Kofi's hand on her thigh.

"That's your sister, Kofi," Kara said with a smirk. Her parents and Kofi laughed, but Shae glanced at Sheldon just in time to see annoyance flash across his face before he fixed it into an expression she couldn't read.

CHAPTER FIVE

"You have the option of telling me what your fucking problem is instead of just sitting there stewing in whatever crawled up your ass."

Kofi reached to the coffee table and muted the Premier League football match they'd returned to Sheldon's house to watch. Sheldon had been in a pissy mood since halfway through Shae's birthday brunch and Kofi was over it. He and Sheldon made plans to come back to the house he rented with Kara after Shae's brunch to chill since the night before. He'd looked forward to catching up with Sheldon while they watched football and drank a few beers. Kofi considered scrapping the plans altogether when Sheldon started acting the fool but figured his friend would snap out of it. Sheldon hadn't and Kofi wished he'd just gone back to his hotel. He would've been having a cocktail while chilling by the pool instead of trying to resist the urge to punch his best friend in his face for being a dick. Kofi tried to keep the edge from his voice but he wasn't sure he was successful. At this rate, he didn't give a damn.

"We're good," Sheldon said although Kofi was sure his best friend's jaw was about to snap under the pressure of how tightly he was clenching it. Sheldon tried to reach for the remote, but Kofi turned off the TV. He knew what Sheldon's problem was and it was about time they had a conversation about it. He couldn't understand Sheldon's insistence that he stayed away from Shae. It didn't seem rooted in any fear that he wasn't good enough for her or might hurt her.

"You're losing your mind because I told Shae to save a dance for me? Run that back through your head and make it make sense."

"We spoke about this already," Sheldon said.

Kofi sucked his teeth. "Yeah. It was ridiculous then too. Shae isn't a baby. Besides, I asked for a dance not to go balls deep in her."

An image of him doing just that flashed across his mind and Kofi's mouth went dry. He wondered if the same image accosted Sheldon because he looked a little sick before he glared at Kofi. If looks could kill, he'd be a dead man.

"I'm not an idiot. I know you have the hots for my little sister."

The accusation pulled Kofi up short. Despite Sheldon's warnings, Kofi never thought Sheldon believed he was attracted to Shae. *Attracted to Shae*. He almost laughed at that. He was far more than attracted to Shae. He wasn't going to let Sheldon know that though.

"What are you talking about?"

Sheldon scoffed. "You obviously don't remember the way you behaved when she came to Jamaica for UWI's Carnival."

Kofi had been half expecting Sheldon to speak about all the time he and Shae spent together during that Christmas almost four years ago. He was shocked he went that far back in history. He didn't remember behaving any way other than normal when an eighteen-year-old Shae visited them at University to check out the campus she'd intended to attend while enjoying the yearly campus Carnival.

"Honestly, Sheldon, what are you talking about? Winston was the one you almost had to beat off of Shae with a stick."

"But you were always staring like a damned stalker. It was annoying as shit."

Kofi couldn't remember doing that but he knew Sheldon's recollection was probably accurate. He had been thoroughly unprepared for the Shae that walked out of Norman Manley International Airport's arrival lounge in ass hugging jeans and a tube top that covered breasts that seemed like they'd fit perfectly in his hands. Thinking of Shae in such a sexual manner was startling, but all of that melted away when she spotted him and Sheldon waiting for her at the taxi stand. Her russet-colored eyes brightened and her face broke into the widest, most beautiful smile. His chest felt tight, even now a decade later, when he thought about that moment. Kofi turned to Sheldon, whose eyes still flashed with annoyance, with an argument on the tip of his tongue. He almost started shooting off his mouth but rethought it. It didn't make any sense. He tried to swallow the annoyance he felt. He was only in Antigua for the next two weeks and he hadn't seen Sheldon in at least a year and a half. He wasn't going to spend the entire vacation being at odds with his best friend over something that wouldn't happen. Kofi remembered how Shae's breath hitched when he squeezed her thigh. Well, maybe *wouldn't* was an unnecessarily strong word.

"As your friend I've got to tell you that trying to police every guy who expresses an interest in Shae is creepy and overbearing. She's a grown ass woman."

"You are not *every guy*," Sheldon groused. "You've been around her since she was a little girl and she's had a stupid ass crush on you for half her life. She's like your sister."

Kofi sighed. "Shae is not my sister."

He could see Sheldon getting ready with his comeback, so he held his hand up. "You're wasting your time. I'm not going after your little sister."

The tension around them lifted a fraction. Sheldon cracked a small smile after a few minutes. "I didn't think you would. You're my best friend and I trust you. I know you wouldn't betray me like that."

Kofi thought of the way his dick instantly hardened when Shae sauntered into the restaurant looking sweet, but sexy as hell in that alluring ass dress that made him think of how easy it would be to bunch it up around her hips and slide into her. He reached to the coffee table for the cold, Wadadli beer and took a large sip as if it could cool the fire that raged inside him.

I know you wouldn't betray me like that.

Kofi hoped Sheldon wasn't willing to bet on that.

CHAPTER SIX

Shae turned her back to her full-length mirror and tossed a look over her shoulder so she could properly observe her outfit. The theme of the party was mid-90s to mid-2000s dancehall, so Shae figured wearing *pum pum* shorts would fit quite nicely. She grinned as she admired how the ridiculously short, black jeans hugged her apple shaped butt and showed a bit of ass cheek. She paired them with a cropped gold bustier, which left her dangling belly button ring on display. Shae fluffed her twist outs before she brushed a deep, purple matte lipstick on her lips.

"Thirty looks *gooood* on you."

Jada appeared behind her in white shorts and a red blouse with a deep V cut in the front.

"I had to try a thing," she laughed.

Her best friend smirked. "As if you have to try. Kofi won't know what hit him."

"You are such an instigator," Shae complained. "Nothing is happening there."

"Why not? Birthday sex doesn't count."

Shae rolled her eyes. "I don't know where you learned math,

Jada, but I'm sure it doesn't work like that. Kofi is a dead end anyway, he isn't even into me like that."

She tasted the lie in her words as soon as she spoke them. She remembered the look in his eyes when he hugged her goodbye and reminded her she promised to save a dance for him. Lust. Shae sighed. Then again, this wasn't the first time she'd gotten carried away and read things into Kofi's actions that simply weren't there.

"Even if he was interested," she continued, reaching for the set of actions she *knew* she was reading correctly. "I feel like Sheldon has warned him off me. He almost flipped out at breakfast today when it seemed like Kofi was flirting with me."

Jada screwed up her face and rolled her eyes. "That isn't a good look on Sheldon's corny ass. Did I tell you about the time he tried to make a pass at me?"

Shae laughed. "Only a thousand times."

Jada pulled her locs out of the rubber band that held them and let them fall down her back. She leaned closer to the mirror and put on the finishing touches of makeup before she said, "Don't wait for Kofi to make a move on you. Shoot your birthday shot."

"I can't..."

Jada held her shoulders and made a production of shaking them. "Do it for the culture, bitch. That man doesn't even have big dick energy. He has *biggest* dick energy. You owe it to me. I volunteer you and your pussy as tribute."

"Have I ever told you I can't stand you?" Shae asked, even though she was laughing so hard she almost wheezed.

Jada winked. "Only ten times today."

She smacked Shae's ass as she started walking off. "Shoot your shot, Shae Marie Abbott. Make mama proud."

"WELCOME TO YOUR BIRTHDAY."

Jada grabbed Shae's arm and guided her into her parents' yard before untying the blindfold she insisted Shae wore. Shae's mouth fell open. The hedges were all wrapped in fairy lights and paper lanterns hung from the branches of the tamarind and mango trees. Lights lined the walkway up to the wrap-around porch. It was so much more whimsical and ethereal than Shae expected. Jada outdid herself. Shae smiled so hard her cheeks burned as she turned and pulled her friend into an excited hug.

"This is gorgeous," she whispered, fighting the emotion clogging her throat. "This is more than I expected. Thank you."

"We got all the set up footage just in case you wanted to make a vlog out of it," Jada said. "I'm pretty damn good in front of the camera if I do say so myself."

"You're amazing."

Jada laughed and flipped her locs over her shoulder. "I thought you couldn't stand me."

She didn't give Shae a chance to respond but instead ushered her up the steps. "Are you ready for your thirtieth birthday party?"

Shae felt a little silly at how giddy she was but she couldn't help the small bounces in her steps as she moved towards the door. She was late by design and expected the party to be in full swing but things seemed suspiciously quiet. Jada swung the door open to reveal about sixty of her friends standing around in the cleared out living room and dining room as if they'd been waiting for her.

"Happy Birthday," they all yelled while the DJ started playing Trap Beckham's 'Birthday Bitch'. She laughed and started moving her hips as Trap reminded her she was a bad bitch and it was her duty to fuck things up in the worst way because it was her birthday. Her friends egged her on as she allowed her inner ratchet to come out. She was still twerking to her heart's content when Raelynn came sauntering out of the kitchen with a chocolate cake with sparklers on top. Brianna followed behind her with a bottle of Jose Cuervo in one hand and a bottle of Chandon in the other.

"Make a wish," Raelynn said, pushing the cake towards Shae. She blew out the candle and tried to not think too hard about the fact Kofi's face popped into her mind instantly. She scanned the darkened room and her heart flipped when she spotted him leaning up against the wall nearest to the hallway with Sheldon at his side.

"It's time to get birthday drunk," Jada shouted in her ear. She reluctantly pulled her attention away from Kofi to Jada, who was grabbing the champagne from Brianna. The crowd cheered as Jada popped the bottle and encouraged Shae to tilt her head backwards so she could pour a generous amount down her throat. She barely gave Shae time to recover before she was doing the same with the tequila.

"With that," the DJ said. "Let's get this party started."

CHAPTER SEVEN

Kofi knew he should pull his attention from Shae, especially after the tense conversation he'd had with Sheldon earlier that day. But how the hell could he when she walked into the party looking like *that*? He got to the party about twenty minutes before, trying to downplay how anxious he was to lay eyes on Shae again. People were vibing, grabbing generously poured drinks from the bar set up in the kitchen and waiting for the birthday girl to make her appearance. And what a fucking appearance that was. He was just getting over how her outfit seemed designed to show off her body in ways that had him instantly hard when she started playfully twerking to the song the DJ played to announce her arrival.

"Jesus," he murmured under his breath, quickly trying to cover it with a cough when Sheldon looked suspiciously in his direction. Kofi wasn't used to feeling out of control. It was uncomfortable and unnerving for him. He watched Shae's playful interactions with her friends with a smile but when she blew out her candles and started scanning the room as if she was looking for something... only stopping when her eyes landed on him, Kofi accepted he was in a whole fucking heap of trouble.

THE PARTY WAS MORE entertaining than half the clubs he'd been to in the last several years. The DJ kept dropping tune after tune and they were all laced with nostalgia. He now understood why Shae wanted her party to only play dancehall songs from the mid-90s to the mid-2000s. The crowd erupted into cheers so loud when the DJ started playing the opening strains of Voicemail's 'Wacky Dip' that he had to stop and pull the song up from the start. Kofi joined the persons who moved towards the middle of the room as they launched into the song's choreographed dance that used to provide so much entertainment at parties while they were growing up. Urged on from the reaction, the DJ played several more songs with popular dances and Kofi danced until he was sweating. He disappeared to the kitchen to get a drink to cool him down when he ran into Shae. She and Jada were hanging around the island sipping their drinks as they casually danced to the music. He couldn't take his eyes off Shae as she moved her hips in tight circles while T.O.K encouraged her to shake her *bam bam*. She grinned widely when she saw him. "Oh hey, Kofi. Having fun?"

He wanted to reach out and run his hand through her hair but stopped short and put his hands in his pockets instead.

"Maybe too much fun. I'm just coming to get another English Harbour and Coke."

"Or," she suggested. "You can have a few birthday shots with me."

Jada smirked. "Yeah. She's been thinking about shooting birthday shots."

A look passed between them that he didn't understand, but he saddled up to the island anyway as Jada poured six shot glasses filled with tequila. She pushed three glasses towards Kofi and the other three towards Shae before she mentioned needing to check on something and hurried out the kitchen like it was on fire. Kofi chuckled. That look was suddenly clear.

Shae winced as she took a shot. "Jada's dramatic. Don't read too much into it."

He took his first shot and laughed. "So she isn't trying to set us up?"

Shae took her second shot and immediately followed it with the third before she finally brought her eyes to his. Damn. She was so fucking gorgeous. "She thinks I should proposition you."

He laughed when it clicked. "Shoot your birthday shot?"

"Yes."

He took two steps towards her, not caring that Sheldon could walk into the kitchen and throw a fit. He held her waist, resisting the temptation to slide his hands downwards to cup her ass. Barely.

"Shoot your shot, Shae Butter," he said. Her mouth parted slightly as her eyes darted to his lips. Kofi wondered if she would have the nerve. He didn't have to wonder long. Shae pushed her body into him, rose to her toes and brushed those full, sexy lips against his. He groaned against her as he gave his hands the permission to go where they had been dying to go. Her ass felt so good against his palms. Kofi pressed his lips harder against her open mouth as his tongue stroked the insides of her mouth. She wasn't shy about kissing him back and soon the loud, heavy dancehall beat was merely background noise as he pulled her closer to him. A startled sound escaped her throat when she felt his erection for the first time. He pulled away and grinned. He was unashamed that it was so obvious how badly she affected him but it still took a few seconds to find his breath before he whispered, "Damn."

CHAPTER EIGHT

Shae grabbed the edges of the countertop and stared at herself in the bathroom mirror. She giggled. Was she really doing this? Kissing Kofi ignited the fire that had been slowly smoldering inside her and she'd known instantly that kissing him wasn't enough... couldn't be enough. She'd closed her eyes and remembered Jada's wild ass telling her to shoot her birthday shot. And so she did. She'd pulled away from Kofi with lips still vibrating from how roughly they were kissing and asked him to meet her in the small half bathroom at the end of the hall. She'd held her breath while she waited for his response. When he grabbed her by the waist and pulled her in for another searing kiss that had her pussy throbbing, she knew she'd made the right decision.

"Say less," he said, before telling her he would give her a head start. That was five minutes ago and Shae tried to control her breathing and anticipation. She didn't do a good job at either. She jumped when the bathroom door swung open as if she hadn't been expecting him. He was on her before she could blink. His lips pressed against to hers, urgently and roughly as she brought her shaking hands to the back of his head to pull him closer. It still wasn't enough. He squeezed her ass and smacked it. Shae pulled her head back and stared at him. She was unable to catch her breath. Unable to make her heart slow down. Unable to wrap her head around what was happening.

"What?" he asked, stroking his thumb across her cheek. Shae shook her head with a smile thinking of how many nights she'd gone to sleep wondering how it would feel to kiss him.

"I just never imagined I'd ever get to do this."

He chuckled. "Neither did I."

He ran his thumb down the side of her neck and gently placed the rest of his fingers on the other side. She answered the question in his eyes by tilting her chin upwards, welcoming the squeeze as he brought his lips to hers. She kissed him greedily, sighing into his open-mouthed kiss as his tongue crashed against hers. Her pussy didn't know what to do with her damn self. Shae's hands went to her shorts and she struggled to pull them down, almost melting with relief when Kofi helped her. She wasn't sure exactly what she needed but she knew it involved him being pressed against, on or in her body. He pushed her against the counter before dropping to his knees and nudging her legs open with his head. In that instant, all of Shae's prayers were answered. Kofi grabbed her thighs as he swiped his tongue vertically across her slit before finding her clit and sucking on it. She cried out when he sucked her even harder before he straightened his tongue out and slid it inside her. She grabbed the back of his head, thankful his hair was grown out just enough for her to grip it firmly as he fucked her with his tongue. She bucked against him. Kofi ran his hands lightly up and down her hips and thighs before he grabbed her waist and held her in place as he continued to push her to the brink with each firm stroke of his tongue. He came up for air just as she thought she would die from it all.

"Open wider for me," he said. She didn't need to be told

twice. "God," he breathed. "You're everything I imagined and more."

Everything I imagined. Shae's pussy throbbed and gushed a little at the thought of Kofi fantasizing about her. He pulled her clit into his mouth and sucked lightly and then grazed it just hard enough for her to cry out.

"Again," she moaned. He flicked his tongue against her a few times and sucked gently before pulling back slightly and blowing a light stream of air on her throbbing clit. She was just adjusting to the abrupt shift in sensation when he took her in his mouth again, grazing his teeth against her just like she'd begged him to. A strangled cry lodged in her throat as she felt the first stirrings of an orgasm deep in her belly. She tried pulling him closer to her, but he turned his head and placed light kisses against her inner thigh instead. Her pussy protested. Heavily.

"Kofi," she moaned. She gasped when he removed his head from between her legs altogether and starting standing up. A protest formed on her lips but before she could utter a word he was fisting his hand through her hair and pulling her up to meet his lips. He kissed her with the kind of aggression that had her moaning in his mouth and sinking her teeth into his lips as her fingers moved towards her clit on their own accord. He gently grabbed her wrist and whispered against her cheek. "Don't you dare..."

"I was so close," she whined.

He chuckled. "I know. Don't worry. I got you. Turn around for me."

Shae turned to face the mirror as Kofi lifted one of her legs across the granite countertop.

"Shae Butter?" he whispered as he slowly stroked the inside of her folds. His touch was feather light, but Shae wanted to jump out of her skin.

"Mhmm?" She didn't trust her vocal cords to form words.

He continued with the feather like probing while he leaned forward and drew her earlobe into his mouth. Shae shivered.

"Hold tight."

Her already fuzzy brain had barely processed his warning before Kofi plunged a thick finger into her pussy. She clenched around him and almost flew face first into the sink when he made a hooking motion and flicked against a spot that had her arching her back wildly towards him. Kofi held her waist to stabilize her before repeating his warning to hold on tight. Her belly tightened in anticipation of whatever it was he was about to do to her. He continued stroking that spot until Shae was ready to climb the walls. She panted and moaned as her entire body fell captive to his handiwork. Shae raised her head and gasped. She barely recognized the dazed woman looking back at her in the mirror. Her lips were swollen, her eyes hooded with lust and her hair in more disarray than a wig in a Tyler Perry movie. She looked well and thoroughly fucked, and Shae didn't even know what his dick looked like yet.

"You like that?" he breathed when his other hand found her clit and moved in quick, tight circles. Shae didn't answer him. How could she? Not when he was literally trying to finesse her soul from her body. He added a second finger and increased the pressure but kept his strokes maddeningly languid, his fingers grazing against that tiny spot that drove her wild. Her stomach coiled tightly. She tried to keep her eyes open but she couldn't manage it. She didn't have the strength. All that mattered was that maddening vortex of pleasure that seemed to expand with every stroke until it consumed her. He continued stroking her firmly, but slowly, before moving his other hand from her clit to trace his fingers lightly down her spine. She let out a ragged breath and tried to grip the edges of the bathroom counter more tightly. She could feel her orgasm building and she wasn't sure she could handle it. She squirmed against his finger and bit down on her lip tightly, as if the sharp burst of pain would stop the impending tornado of pleasure from ripping through her. It did fuck all. She could feel Kofi's tongue slowly tracing the path his finger had taken down her spine before he planted soft kisses against each ass cheek. And then suddenly her clit was in his mouth again. He alternated between sucking and grazing until she thought she would go mad. And perhaps she did. Shae couldn't remember having a single coherent thought when he stopped stroking her pussy and started rocking his fingers from side to side, increasing the speed and pressure until Shae's body started shaking. He strummed her clit with his tongue to match the rhythm of his fingers. Shae tried fighting against the pleasure she felt, but soon accepted it was a losing battle. So she embraced it. She couldn't think straight. She couldn't breathe. Her vision started closing in on her and when Kofi grazed his teeth over her swollen, throbbing clit, she exploded. She was grateful as hell for the loud ass music because her throat ached from how much she screamed. Kofi continued sucking her and stroking her pussy until she begged him to stop. She tried to bring her shaking leg to the floor and turn around to face Kofi but it took two attempts for how badly it shook. She couldn't even be mad about the smug look on his face. He earned that shit. It took a while before Shae's heart slowed down enough for her to breathe properly again. As her thoughts slowly became less jumbled, Shae knew there was only one thing in the world she wanted to do. Wipe that smug look off of Kofi's face. Her hands went to his pants, unbuckling his belt as his eyes widened.

She grinned up at Kofi before easing his pants and boxers down and dropping to her knees, impressed as hell when his dick sprang free. Jada wasn't so far off the mark. She took a bit of him in her mouth, enjoying the way he felt on her tongue. She eased back and looked up at him. "Kofi?"

"Yes?"

It sounded like the word was dragged from his throat and Shae smiled more widely. "Hold tight."

CHAPTER NINE

Hold tight.

Kofi chuckled at the teasing lilt to her voice, but he should have listened to her. He hadn't been prepared for her to nearly swallow him whole.

Goddamn.

The whimper left his lips before he could stop it as he squeezed his eyes shut and fisted his hands through her hair. Then, he made the mistake of opening them and looking down at Shae. Her eyes watered as she took in more of his dick and fondled his balls while touching herself as she kneeled with her legs spread wide. He breathed hard when she slowly eased his dick from her mouth, spat on its head and started stroking him in firm, twisting motions. He groaned. She cocked her head to the side and continued pleasuring him with her hand before she leaned forward and placed a chaste kiss at the tip of his dick's head. He chuckled. Shae was always goofy as hell, and he was happy she hadn't grown out of that. She met his eyes again as she took his dick all the way down her throat and hummed. And then she took him deeper.

"Jesus," he groaned. Did this woman not have a gag reflex?

She seemed encouraged by his reaction, stroking him harder and taking him deeper until Kofi couldn't hold back anymore. He finally took her advice and gripped the edge of the counter as the orgasm shot through him and he emptied himself into her mouth. She swallowed it easily and continued sucking as if she hadn't already almost taken his life with that mouth.

"You're killing me here," he groaned. She drew away with mischief in her eyes. "Good."

He helped her from the floor, grabbing her waist and wiping away the remnants of his orgasm that coated her lips.

"As much as I want to take this further," he said, trying to suppress the disappointment he felt. "People must be looking for you."

She glanced at her reflection in the mirror and sighed. "You're right. I need to put myself together. Rain check?"

He kissed her neck. "I definitely plan to collect."

KOFI WAS ONLY two steps out of the bathroom when he ran into Sheldon.

"Where have you been?"

"What? You missed me?" he teased. He glanced behind him, hoping Shae was still busy trying to put herself together. He tapped Sheldon's shoulder and gestured towards the kitchen, relieved as hell when he followed him without questions. He was still buzzing from the feel of Shae's mouth against him and the hint of the taste of her pussy that remained on his tongue. He didn't want an argument with Sheldon to ruin any of that. He shoved away memories of Shae and found Sheldon looking at him with his eyebrows drawn together.

"What?"

"Where were you?" his friend asked again. "Your breath smells like pussy."

He was about to shoot off a smart-ass comment when Jada stalked up to them with two cups in her hand. She thrust one toward Kofi. "Anybody see the birthday girl? Been looking for her for a good twenty minutes now."

"I haven't," Sheldon said. He cast a glance at Kofi. "Have you?"

Was that an edge in his voice? Kofi raised his eyebrow.

"Where have you been?" Jada suddenly asked. He looked past Sheldon to see Shae wandering over. She looked... *disheveled,* and memories of her spread wide against the bathroom counter made him go hard.

"It's my party and I disappear if I want to," Shae said in a sing-song voice. "What did I miss?"

"More shots," Jada said with a smirk. She looked from Shae to Kofi and her smirk widened. "Unless you've already had all your shots for the night."

"I'm still game." Shae finally brought her eyes to his. "How about you guys?"

"I was actually looking for Kofi to tell him that Kara and I are heading out."

Shae crinkled her nose and laughed out loud. "It's been years and you guys are still leaving parties halfway through to screw each other's brains out? Grow up!"

Sheldon pulled her into a hug. "Whatever, brat. Be safe and don't let Jada give you alcohol poisoning."

He and Sheldon bumped fists and then his best friend was off in search of his fiancée. Kofi was... relieved. It wasn't even two in the morning so the party was still going pretty strong. He wrapped his hands around Shae's waist and pulled her into him. "What about that dance you promised me?"

CHAPTER TEN

Shae knew she would pay for everything in the morning, but she didn't care. She'd had so many expectations for her thirtieth birthday but this surpassed them all. She rocked and rolled her hips to the heavy, old school dancehall reggae beats, screaming with excitement every time the DJ played a song she loved but hadn't heard in years. The entire bottom floor of her parents' house took on the kind of feel that only a packed, sweaty house party could. A fete couldn't compete and neither could a nightclub. Jada worked the floor expertly, making sure Shae always had a drink in her hand. And then there was Kofi. Shae circled the floor, dancing with a few of her friends every so often so that people didn't start asking questions, but she spent most of the rest of the party glued to Kofi. The feel of the hard planes of his body against her back and his big hands cupping her thighs and lower abdomen as their bodies moved in tandem to songs they probably had no business listening to at twelve and fifteen did crazy things to her libido. She couldn't stop the wide smile from spreading across her face when Kofi buried his face in her neck and starting singing along to Wayne Wonder's 'No Letting Go'.

Shae couldn't count the number of times she dreamed of Kofi singing the song about a man promising his lover that they would be together forever to her. Shae chuckled, wondering if she would wake up and realize this was all a dream. Kofi pulled her closer and she gasped at how generous his dick felt pressed up against her. No. This was very, very real. She spun around so she was facing him, still moving her hips in slow, undulating motions before she tiptoed up to him and whispered against his ear, "Let's get out of here."

He squeezed her waist. "It's your party."

"And I want to fuck you."

Jada would have been proud as hell if she witnessed that little exchange. Kofi licked his lips and grabbed her ass. "We've got time, Shae Butter."

Shae glanced around them. The room was dark but from what she could make out, people were too busy dancing to DJ's set to be paying much attention to her and Kofi in the corner. Emboldened by liquor... or lust... or both, Shae ran her hand down his chest and into his jeans. She cupped his dick. "I want to fuck you."

"Shae..."

She massaged him and smiled when he hardened instantly under her touch. "I'll be in my room."

Shae's heart thumped hard as she turned away from him and made her way to the kitchen where she poured herself a drink.

"Everything okay?"

She turned to Jada and smiled nervously. "Never been better."

HE WASN'T GOING to follow her. Kofi held on to that conviction for less than half of a second after he watched Shae and her ass sashay away. Who was he trying to fool? There was no way he'd be able to turn down getting closer to Shae. Not now he knew what she tasted like, felt like, and how she responded to his touch. He waited a while, the room suddenly hotter than it was minutes ago, before he navigated the familiar path to Shae's old bedroom. She was topless and wiggling out of her shorts when he pushed the door open. He closed it softly, even though he didn't have to with how loudly the music was playing downstairs. Kofi started moving towards Shae but stopped short. He stood there for a while, admiring the way she looked standing bathed in the moonlight. Her head was tilted to the side while she moved seductively to the music. The DJ knew the party was wrapping up and had started playing the kind of songs that encouraged people to leave with each other. Shae ran her hands down her belly to her thighs as she danced. Kofi was so hard he could barely breathe. He kept his eyes focused on her ass as he moved closer to her. He was a few steps away when she turned around and locked her gaze on his as she picked up the pace she rolled her hips. She closed the distance between them until her breasts were pressed hard against his chest. He squeezed her ass and pulled her into him, not even trying to swallow the groan in his throat. She tipped her head up and he crashed his mouth against hers. Kofi sucked on Shae's lips before he caressed her tongue with his own while he massaged her ass cheeks. She melted into him, bringing her hands to the back of his neck to pull him closer. The intensity of Shae's kisses made his blood run hot. Kofi spun her around, splaying his hand across her stomach and pulling her against him. His other hand massaged her breasts—twisting and pulling at her nipples as he kissed her neck. She squirmed, but he kept her pressed tightly against him. He was right. Shae's breasts fit perfectly in the palms of his hands. She smelled faintly of the sweat from dancing and her arousal. Kofi's body tightened. He continued playing with her nipples as his other hand moved lower towards her sex. He cupped her warmth and glided his fingers between her wet folds for a few seconds before he slid a finger inside. She clenched around him as he worked her over. She was so damn responsive. Kofi could spend forever pleasuring her with his fingers, enjoying the way she arched her back into him and how her body shook, but he ached for her. He continued his steady rhythm, using his free hand to explore her body – a pinch of a nipple there, fingertips brushed across her ribcage, a gentle squeeze of her throat as he worked her towards an orgasm. She came violently – body shuddering, back arching and ass pressed hard into his crotch. He held her against him as she came down off the high of her orgasm – dragging his lips along her earlobes and her neck. Shae shimmied out of his embrace, tugged on the hem of his shirt and helped him pull it over his head. She went for his pants next with urgency that matched the complete loss of self-control he felt. She stroked his dick before he covered her hand and pushed it away. He was already barely holding on to control and he wasn't going to embarrass himself by nutting before they even got started. She cocked her head to the side and grinned at him before she turned and walked the short distance to her bed. Kofi didn't know what he expected, but he sure as hell wasn't prepared for Shae to climb on the bed and bend over for him – back perfectly arched and that cute, fat ass in the air.

"Fuck," he whispered under his breath as he held her waist, rubbing his dick against her slit a few times before he sank into her. He squeezed his eyes shut as he buried himself to the hilt inside her before he drew himself out and slammed into her again. Her pussy clenched him in her hot wetness and Kofi felt his control slip a notch. He stroked her back as his thrusts deepened and picked up pace. He hated that the music was so damn loud because he wanted nothing more than to hear her moan. He massaged her hips and ass as he pulled her into him. He slammed into her over and over again, and just when Kofi felt in control again, Shae threw him off. She looked back at him with the moonlight bathing her face and smiled. Then she started throwing that ass back at him. He groaned as she set her own pace and depth, his eyes focused on how her ass bounced as she moved. Kofi fisted his hand in her hair and carefully pulled her back towards him. He let her take control for a while before he pulled out and turned her around. He wanted to see her face when she came. His dick protested immediately and his body shook when he finally slid back into her. She felt like home, but Kofi wasn't going to think about that now. He wouldn't think about anything other than how amazing she felt against him as he slammed into her. Shae wrapped her legs around him as he picked up his pace, keeping his eyes trained on her. He brought his lips to hers as he switched it up, moving in circular motions instead. He quickened the movements when she tightened her legs around him. Kofi could feel her body starting to shake under him so he kissed her neck, shoulder and collarbone as he continued moving faster. She raised her hips, matching his circles with her own for a few seconds before her entire body stiffened and she started shaking even harder. He squeezed her nipples while he thrust hard and quick as he chased his own release. It wasn't long before he couldn't hold out anymore. He brought his lips to hers, trying to drown his groans in the kiss as he came. He wasn't sure how long he stayed collapsed on her before he rolled off, giving her some room to breathe. It was only then he realized the music had all but stopped. Shae grinned and sang, *"Happy birthday to me"* and his heart thudded against his chest. There was something between them. Something electric and worth exploration. Sheldon's angry face flashed through his mind but Kofi didn't care. He was done running from his feelings.

CHAPTER ELEVEN

Shae woke up throbbing.

She'd roused once before, snuggled into Kofi in her childhood bed as sunlight started creeping into her room. He'd kissed the side of her head, murmured something about it being safer for him to leave, and promised to message her. She wasn't even surprised she'd fallen back to sleep with the amount of liquor flowing through her veins.

Her birthday party was the most beautiful blur but there were some parts Shae remembered vividly. She could almost feel Kofi's warm tongue lapping against her clit and she smiled when she remembered how his head lolled backwards just before he came. She brought her hand to her pussy, biting on the corner of her bottom lip as she pictured Kofi in her mind. She'd thought nothing could top their tryst in the bathroom but she'd been so wrong. She still ached pleasantly where she'd stretched to take him. Shae brushed her hand over her clit and moaned as she repeated the movement. She'd known sex with Kofi would be amazing. There was no way he could eat her out like *that*, have a dick like *that*, have sex appeal like *that* and not know how to use it to his advantage. She squeezed her clit between her thumb and index finger—rubbing it slowly as she called to her mind how he felt inside her. She couldn't help the breathy moan that spilled from her parted lips as she arched her back. Her fingers were a sad substitute for just how well Kofi worked her over but they'd have to do. The orgasm hit Shae hard, forcing all the breath from her lungs as she screamed out Kofi's name. She'd barely started coming down from her high when her cell phone started blaring Beyonce. She sat up in bed wondering where the hell her phone was before she remembered she'd undressed as soon as she'd entered the bedroom.

"Yes, Jada?" she whined when she answered.

"Was it Kofi I saw leaving here at the butt crack of dawn?"

"Maybe."

"You're welcome."

She laughed. "What?"

"You're obviously too properly dicked down to remember your manners, but it's okay. I forgive you. I'm happy you listened to me because as we know..."

"You're always right," Shae said with another laugh. "Give me a few. I'll be right down."

Jada was a trip and a half but Shae was so lucky to have her in her life. She fished around her room and found a pair of yoga pants and a large T-shirt from the last time she spent the night at her parents' house.

She found Jada in the kitchen firing off commands at the group of young men she'd hired to help put the house back in order. Jada turned the camera she was holding to Shae and said, "Here's Shae Butter. Worse for the wear, but alive... and glowing."

"Stop it!" she protested, reaching for the camera.

"I want every nasty detail," Jada said once she double-checked to make sure the camera was turned off. She pointed Shae to her hangover cure laid out on the table; a few ibuprofens, Alka-Seltzer, black coffee and toast. Her stomach lurched. The fun she had the night before didn't come without consequences. She swallowed the pills and nibbled on the toast until she started feeling better. Then she turned to her friend and did just what she asked. Shae gave Jada every nasty detail.

CHAPTER TWELVE

Kofi stepped into the steaming shower and allowed the hot water to rain down on his back. He couldn't get Shae out of his mind. If someone had tried to convince him he'd ever get as close to Shae as he had... Kofi would have laughed in their face. He smiled as he remembered the way her forehead crinkled and how she chewed on her bottom lip just before she came. He was hard just thinking about her. It didn't surprise Kofi that his lust for her burned brighter. What he and Shae shared the night before was exceptional. Still wanting her was only natural but his body wasn't the only thing on edge. He was feeling tenderness too. It was the same feeling that had knocked him for ten when he watched her smile at him and Sheldon all those years ago and again when he dropped her home after Nocturnal. The lust he could handle. He couldn't handle wanting more. Wanting more of what? Kofi couldn't even answer that. He thought about what he could possibly expect from Shae throughout his shower and the late lunch he had in the hotel's main dining room.

He was scrolling through his phone getting ready to message Shae when his phone chimed with an incoming message from the last person he expected to contact him. His mother. Well, the woman who gave birth to him.

Deborah Matthews-Callahan was a lot of things, but she'd never been much of a mother. Not really. Not truly. That was why he spent so much time at the Abbotts while he was growing up in the first place.

"I hear you're on the island," his mother said. Annoyance dripped like acid from her voice, but Kofi was way past giving a damn.

"I am."

He didn't offer any more information because he wasn't interested in keeping the conversation going longer than it needed to. His whereabouts were none of her business.

"You could've told me you were coming," she continued. "I had to find out about it from somebody who saw you at Grace's place. They thought you were staying here."

"I got a hotel," he said.

"You could have stayed here."

"Why the hell would I do that? For show? I was barely welcome at that house when I should've been. I'm good." Kofi felt the anger brewing but quickly checked it. He'd decided a while ago that it wasn't worth it. It was never worth it.

"Kofi…"

"I've got to go," he said. "Tell your husband hi."

He disconnected the call and spent some time willing his emotions back under control. He continued scrolling through his phone for Shae's number once he started feeling more grounded. She answered on the fourth ring, sounding just the way he expected after the night she'd had. He chuckled.

"You struggling, aren't you?"

"Stop shouting," she whimpered. "Why do you sound like you're fine?"

"I didn't drink half as much as you did. You took getting

birthday drunk seriously. You think you could manage facing the world?"

"I might," she said after a brief pause. "Depends on what you have in mind?"

"Drinks."

"You can't be serious," Shae said. Kofi laughed at the abject horror in her voice as he told her the best way to get over a hangover was to just keep drinking. Shae was having none of it.

"How about we go to the beach?" he suggested. "We can grab some coconut waters on the way. It should help more than staying curled into bed willing yourself to die."

"I can be ready in an hour," she said. "It'll probably take me that long to get my ass out of bed."

"Send me the directions," he said and then after a pause. "I can't wait to see you."

He wasn't lying. Anticipation settled in his stomach and chased away the last of the negative emotions that surfaced after the phone call with his mother.

He'd settled into bed with the book he'd brought to keep him company when his phone lit up with a message.

Sheldon: Wanna shoot some hoops?

Kofi: Can't. I got plans. Let me hit you up tomorrow."

Sheldon: Plans? Tell me more.

Kofi: Eventually. For now, I'm gonna play it close to my chest.

Kofi dropped his phone on the bed, wondering if he should've just been upfront with Sheldon. He disregarded the thought almost as soon as it entered his mind. Sheldon was going to flip the fuck out. He could take the easy way out and cut whatever was starting between him and Shae short, but he didn't want to. Sex between them had been great but that was not what propelled him to ask her to hang out. He wanted to understand the tender feelings expanding in his chest. He thought about the eventual blow up he'd have to face with Sheldon but pushed it to the side. Kofi decided taking the risk was more important than never knowing.

SHAE WAS ALREADY WAITING for him on her porch when he pulled up to her house a few hours later. Kofi would never admit it out loud, but he was nervous as hell. He chuckled at how stupid that made him feel. This was just Shae. The Shae who screamed until she vomited when Sheldon put a plastic snake in her bed as a prank when she was eight. The Shae who tried to convince her parents that she wanted a goat as a pet when she was ten. The Shae whose boyfriend he and Sheldon threatened with bodily harm when he tried to pressure her into sex at sixteen. He scrubbed his hand over his face. Yes, she was *that* Shae. But now she was also the Shae whose nipples went rock hard at the slightest touch. The Shae who bit her lip and scrunched her forehead when she came. The Shae who made his mouth water when he thought of just how amazing her pussy tasted on his tongue. His dick jumped at the memory. Kofi took a swig of water, trying to quench the burning in his stomach. Shae would never be *just* Shae again. He took her in as he cut the car's engine. She pulled her hair back into a careless ponytail and large, dark shades framed her face. She wore a maxi dress and Kofi had to give himself a quick pep talk. Did she know the things the material of those dresses did to her body? She slid into the car and immediately put her hand to her stomach.

"Still feeling fucked up?"

She sighed as she removed the shades and placed them in

her lap. She rubbed her eyes before she whimpered, "Stop shouting."

He laughed softly and squeezed her thigh. "Poor baby."

Kofi felt the shift in the atmosphere in the car before he even glanced back in Shae's direction. She was chewing on her bottom lip and he saw lust burning in her eyes when he finally locked his with hers. He tapped his fingers against the steering wheel, seriously contemplating hauling her back into her house and abandoning the beach. He imagined himself sliding into Shae and was just about to kill the rental's engine when he reined the instinct in. The purpose of them meeting up was to have some time to chill together. He couldn't remember the last time he had a proper conversation with Shae. Hasty Instagram likes, amusing comments and random messages on important dates would never compare to being able to just vibe in her presence. There were so many things he wanted to know. So many things he hoped to learn. He'd watched her grow into this beautiful butterfly and there was no way she was the same as she was that Christmas. He wanted to know how she handled all the things that came with the career she stumbled into and then excelled in. Kofi had tracked her success keenly with a ridiculous amount of pride. As much as she hated to admit it, Shae was a bit of an Internet star.

"Hugs and kisses, Shae Butter, huh?" he smiled at her sideways as he pulled the car out on the road. Shae's laughter was a symphony of happiness.

"You're a fool."

He laughed. "Hey. I'm just saying I feel you owe me a cut or something."

"For coming up with a nickname?"

"A witty play on words that has proven to be immensely marketable," he corrected with a laugh. "That's why you stole it."

"Straight fool," Shae laughed. "But you're not wrong. My first ever sponsor was with a Shea Butter company."

"I'm thinking a fifteen percent cut," he teased.

"Fifteen percent? That's a highway robbery if I've ever seen one. How about I treat you to dinner? A one off at that."

She was still laughing so hard that she had put her hand to her stomach to settle herself.

"Dinner sounds great, but I'll treat you. It'll be a date."

He waited for her to correct him, for her to use the opportunity to clarify that what happened between them at her birthday party was just sex. But she didn't. Instead, she fixed him with a shy smile and said, "A date it is."

CHAPTER THIRTEEN

It'll be a date.

Shae's heart rate shot up, her skin went warm and she felt a little dizzy with anticipation.

She grimaced. God, she was an embarrassing fool. She and Kofi had amazing sex but she should know better. She *did* know better. A good fuck did not a love story make. But damn it, she wished it could. The twelve-year-old girl inside her with the hopeless crush on Kofi was squealing her little ass off at the thought that maybe, just maybe, Kofi might be interested in something more.

You're a whole fool, her mind shot at her. She was reading way too much into his teasing comment. Kofi wasn't interested in anything beyond a vacation fling. She tried to remind herself of that when he reached across and rest his warm, large hand on her thigh.

They decided on a beach which was surprisingly empty given its popularity and the excellent, sunny day. They'd stopped at the side of the road and bought two large bottles of fresh coconut water to help fight the hangover still kicking Shae's ass.

"Straight from the nut," Kofi had grinned when the smiling man used a rusty cutlass to cut a coconut open and fill up a few more empty bottles. Shae was grateful for the chilly coconut water she sipped slowly while they decided on a spot to lie out on the beach towel she'd brought. They chose a spot at the far end of the beach, near small colorful huts that were usually open on days cruise ships docked, offering a variety of jewelry and branded clothing options. She pushed her toes into the white sand and took another deep drink of coconut water as if it could soothe her nerves.

"You good?" he asked. He sat so close their thighs pressed together and Shae had the overwhelming urge to straddle him. She fought it down. Shae hated to be a *so what is happening here* kind of person, but she figured it was something she needed to do. It was best to get everything out in the open so she could manage the expectations of both the freshly minted thirty-year-old and twelve-year-old versions of herself.

"Are we going to talk about it?" she asked. She was well aware that she was being a massive wuss. She could have asked a direct question. She *should* have asked a direct question. Yet, she hedged around it. Kofi took his sweet time taking a drink of his coconut water and her entire body went hot remembering how those lips looked curved around her nipples. She squeezed her eyes shut and pressed herself down against the towel as if it could stop the throbbing.

"Talk about what?"

He said one thing, but the way his gaze bore into her let Shae know he knew damn well what she was talking about.

"Last night," she said, and when her clarification was met with silence she added. "Stop playing, Kofi. You know exactly what I'm talking about."

"What? Your party?" he chuckled. "It was hype. I felt like I was fifteen again. I can't wait to see that vlog. It'll have a shit-load of views."

"Quit playing," she laughed. "You know I'm *not* talking about the party."

He brought his hands to the back of her neck and pulled her towards him. He brushed his lips across hers. "Talking about this?"

It took a while before she even remembered to breathe. "Among other things."

His hand moved under her dress and he cupped her sex. "This?"

Shae squirmed against his hand, biting her tongue to stop the moans from erupting from her mouth. He slid his thumb under her bikini bottoms and strummed Shae's clit until she felt like she would fall apart. She should tell him to stop, but Shae couldn't find it in herself to care that they were on a public beach in the middle of the day when her body succumbed to the orgasm. Stars erupted behind her eyes as she threw her head back and cried out. Kofi was smiling at her when she finally returned to herself.

"You were wrong for that," she muttered, hating the way her cheeks flamed and her breath lodged in her chest.

He chuckled. "Am I? Seemed like I was pretty fucking right a moment ago."

Shae started to fire off the comeback on her tongue but Kofi silenced her by covering her mouth with his. His languid kisses just reignited the fire his touches lit deep in her belly. She broke the kiss and turned her cheek. "Did you invite me out here to get us arrested for public indecency?"

"I'm down if you're down," Kofi responded. He dragged his lips across her cheek and along her jawline. She leaned in to him but he straightened up after a few seconds, reaching for his bottle of coconut water and taking a huge gulp. Shae throbbed as she watched him. It was a small mercy he hadn't pressed the issue because they'd probably be looking at an indecency charge by now.

"I know my actions are probably saying the opposite but I invited you out because I wanted catch up. I haven't chilled with you since you started making yourself scarce because you thought I didn't want to kiss you after Nocturnal all those years ago."

"You say that like I was wrong."

Kofi's brown eyes met hers and he held them for a few seconds before he leaned towards her and kissed her again. "You were."

CHAPTER FOURTEEN

Shae checked to make sure her camera was properly in focus before she set up the shooting lights. She had been prepping to shoot the video she intended to post later that week for a bit over half of an hour. She used the largest spare room in her rental, with its broad windows overlooking the garden and light colored walls, as a shooting room. Shae loved the freedom of having a room dedicated to YouTube videos. She invested more time and energy into her set-ups than she had when she was just shooting in a corner of her bedroom. The first thing she'd done was convert a corner into a space for sit down chats that resembled a talk show. She had a blue loveseat and armchair, a small coffee table with a fluffy rug and plants to add texture. Jada sat on the loveseat, reaching for the glass of wine she was sipping on.

"Let's get this show on the road," she said. "I'm ready to judge you."

Shae laughed. "When *aren't* you judging me?"

Jada placed the wineglass on the coffee table and pulled her locs out of the scrunchie. "I never stop judging but let's focus on this little haul you got going on."

Jada spent the full thirty minutes Shae used setting up the

shoot going in on her for bringing up the *what is happening here* conversation with Kofi. Not that the question ever got answered. It took Shae a while to get over the shock of Kofi admitting he'd wanted to kiss her all those years ago but worried about how Sheldon might react. Once the shock faded away, they spent the rest of the afternoon talking about everything under the sun. He asked her about her career and paid keen attention, asking questions about everything from how she made money to where she got her inspiration and how she survived Antigua's notoriously bad Internet. Shae was accustomed to people treating her career with equal parts fascination and disdain. One date straight up asked when she planned on getting a proper job and another couldn't stop talking about his astonishment that she made so much money from doing what he thought was nothing. She'd ended those situations quickly and was always ready to curse out anyone who tried to get shady with her. She didn't have such issues with Kofi. He was genuinely interested and that made it easy talking to him about her partnerships with different beauty and clothing brands as well as other companies finally wising up to the Caribbean being a hugely untapped market. She'd even partnered with the Grenadian and Cayman Islands tourism boards on campaigns to encourage regional travel. Shae doubled over with laughter when he confessed he'd once gone out on a date with a girl who couldn't stop gushing about her.

"That's when I realized you were famous, babe."

She'd wanted to argue that she was far from famous but couldn't get past the tone of his voice when he called her babe. They spent the rest of the afternoon in the cool, azure waters. Shae tried her best not to read too much into how amazing it felt to be there with her legs wrapped around his waist and arms around his neck as he stroked her back and ass while the waves lapped against them. He told her little things about his life in London, from the job he secured with a top engineering firm before he even finished his Masters in Civil Engineering to his weekend routine of working out before eating back his calories in donuts from his favorite place in Brixton. Jada begged her to just go with the flow and enjoy being with him without heavy expectations, but it was hard. She checked her lighting again and decided Jada was right. They'd have a lot of time to go over what was going on with Kofi after they finished shooting the video. Shae was tapping into a popular YouTube trend where other people rated hauls. She figured it would be an easy video and so she picked out a few bikinis on Zaful, Amazon and Shein. She already filmed herself doing the online shopping, which would be edited into the start of the video. She was still salty as hell about how much she had to pay to get the ten bikinis to Antigua but she had to accept she didn't have the convenience of living in the US. Jada would rank each bikini on a scale of one to ten before providing commentary. There were a bunch of people Shae could've asked to help rate her haul, but she knew Jada would provide insightful and hilarious commentary. The only filter Jada ever used was on Instagram. Shae also set up a photo session with her friend, Brandon, for the next week so she could get some professional photos for her blog and Instagram feed. She would get her money's worth out of those damn bikinis if it was the last thing she did.

"Ready?" she asked Jada as she settled in front of the camera to start her intro.

"Born ready."

Jada took a sip of her wine and struck a pose that had Shae cracking up. It looked like her costar was ready and raring to go. Shae hoped she could keep up and the first step towards that was putting a particular sexy ass man from her mind.

CHAPTER FIFTEEN

Kofi tried to fight the small stirrings of nerves he felt when he raised his fist to Shae's front door and rapped twice. He knew their 'date' only came about because of his teasing, but he put a lot of effort into planning it. He hoped to exceed any expectations Shae might have. That included showing up at the precise time they agreed on with a small box of donuts. He'd gone with the three types he remembered Shae talking about being her favorite in a blog post she'd done to highlight, Donut Ace, a small donut shop in the heart of Saint John. He'd quickly double checked the post before he purchased the red velvet, smores and cinnamon sugar donuts. Kofi first thought of surprising her with flowers but decided against it, knowing Shae would much prefer the donuts. He was about to rap on the door again when she yanked it open. He took a step back as the air rushed from his lungs.

"Goddamn," he murmured. He couldn't tear his eyes away from the beauty in front of him even as he handed her the box of donuts. Her body was a weapon and she dressed to kill. The sleek, yellow pantsuit skimmed her curves and provided a hint of just enough cleavage to make him want to lean forward and bury his face between her breasts. She was so damn beautiful. So damn sexy. So damn soft. She stepped forward into his arms and he slipped his hands around her waist as he buried his face in her neck, inhaling the sweet hints of rose and coconut she liked to wear. He dragged his lips across her neck before he pulled back and crashed them against hers. So damn plump. So damn pliable. So damn sweet. His lips craved hers as soon as he pulled away so he leaned forward and kissed her again.

"You look amazing," he whispered. "I'm kinda ashamed to be seen in public with someone so clearly out of my league."

She slapped her palm against his chest and laughed. "Stop it. You know we will walk into whatever restaurant you chose and women will have little orgasms just looking at you."

"I'm just saying Shae Butter," he grinned. "Who'd have thought your annoying ass would grow up to be the blueprint for perfection."

She couldn't seem to decide whether she wanted to focus on him calling her annoying or the blueprint for perfection. He chuckled as he watched her try to decide. She settled on a bit of both, rolling her eyes as she pulled her bottom lip between her teeth and laughed.

"Whatever, Kofi," she said. "Tell me again why I used to like you so much when I was a kid?"

"Used to?" Kofi said. "You seemed to *like* me a lot a few days ago."

He'd expected her to return his teasing with some of her own. She didn't. Her face softened and she lowered her eyes with a small, shy smile. Kofi grinned. She should be immortalized on canvas and hung in galleries so that the world could be truly blessed with her beauty. The world deserved that. He grinned wider when he considered that, in a way, she landed in a career that allowed for just that. Speaking of career.

"Our reservation starts at six but I thought we could go early so you can get a few photos in," he said. "I looked up the place online and it fits right in with your Instagram aesthetic. That's why I chose it."

Her full lips parted slightly with surprise and he almost leaned forward to kiss it away. He kept himself rooted in place. He needed to exercise self-control and now was as good as a time as any to practice.

"You picked the place based on my Instagram aesthetic?" she asked with a chuckle. "And you adjusted our date time so I could make the best use of the sunlight?"

"I might have," Kofi said, suddenly worried that what seemed like a cute gesture in his head was doing too much. She leaned forward, tipped her chin up and captured his mouth with hers, kissing him softly and pulling away before he could sink into the kiss the way he wanted to.

"Careful," she warned. "A girl could get used to this."

CHAPTER SIXTEEN

He knew how to keep anticipation going. She'd give him that much. Shae still had no idea what they would actually be doing even though Kofi had given her several clues. Not that it mattered too much. She was just excited to spend time with him. She couldn't count the amount of times she'd gone to bed as a teen clutching her favorite teddy bear trying to imagine what it would be like if it was Kofi instead. Shae had given up on trying to control the twelve-year-old inside her who seemed to be on the verge of a breakdown from just how damn excited she was. Never in a million years. Never in her wildest dreams. Never in her most elaborate fantasies had Shae ever imagined that *this* could be happening.

Calm down, she muttered to herself. It wasn't the first time she tried to regain control of her emotions, but it didn't fare any better than her previous attempts.

Kofi hadn't given Shae much to work with when he'd sent her a simple message the day before. *Dress for dinner but bring a bikini.*

She and Jada spent a lot of time rereading those seven words trying to put together an outfit until she gave up and pulled something she'd been looking for a reason to wear out of her closet and called it a day. The way Kofi's eyes roved over her body when she came to the door made her go hot. Kofi had a way of making her feel extremely desirable. She squeezed her thighs together, ever so slightly, to temper the small bursts of lust coursing through her body. Shae wanted to push her body into his and curl herself around him so she could inhale the intoxicating, spicy woodsy scent that was uniquely him but she thought better of it. The date wouldn't happen at all if she moved one step closer to him. She took a small, steadying breath and tried to fight down the soft, seductive voice in her head that whispered, "Fuck the date."

"I'm ready," she said. She disappeared briefly into the kitchen to put up the donuts she would dig into as soon as she got back home before she returned to the door.

"Got anymore hints for me?" she asked once she'd stepped out on the porch.

Kofi shook his head slightly as his lips curved into a smile and Shae almost drowned in the sudden, urgent need to straddle his face.

"Nah," he said. "You have a bikini, right?"

She pointed to the tiny black clutch she held. "Yup."

Kofi's eyes widened as he wet his lips before he stuttered, "It fit? *In there?*"

Her shoulders shook from how hard she laughed. "It does. I only have my vex money in here."

The corners of his mouth tipped upwards. "You walked with vex money?"

His hands went to her lower back as he guided her towards the steps of the porch.

"Come on, Kofi. What West Indian mother didn't teach her daughters to not go anywhere without vex money? My ass isn't putting myself in another person's hands like that. Not even yours."

His hand slid lower until he cupped her ass and squeezed before he leaned down and whispered in her ear. "I hear you, Shae Butter, but I fully expect *this* ass to be in my hands by the end of the night."

The words slid down her spine like a caress. Shae shivered. She lifted her chin so she could look him square in the eyes when she said, "Be nice and you probably won't even have to wait that long."

HE DID GOOD. *Really good.* It didn't take long before Shae knew exactly where they were going. He reached out and held her hand as they entered the lobby of the Cocobay Resort, a sprawling hotel in the south of the island. She knew they were headed to the Sheer Rocks restaurant, which was one of her favorite places. She wondered for a few seconds if perhaps Jada had known more about the date than she let on. She and Kofi continued through the lobby and up the tree-lined path towards the hotel's main pool. The restaurant was located on a bluff overlooking the vast Caribbean Sea and offered stunning sunset views. She had a few photos of her perched on the edge of their plunge pool in bright bikinis with the vivid blue water behind her on her Instagram. She grinned when she remembered Kofi saying he'd come early so she could get photos because the scenery matched her Instagram aesthetic. That impressed her more than anything he could have possibly planned. Many guys found her fun to date for a while but eventually started complaining about all the photos she took, the kind of photos she posted and how she just didn't *turn off*. It became agitating enough that Shae was always hesitant to let people in. That Kofi didn't just understand but also kept her career in his thoughts as he planned their date warmed her all over.

"You've gone all out for something that should have been my treat," she said, turning to smile at Kofi who'd been walking a few steps behind her. Her heart thudded against her chest when their eyes met and he looked at her with a kind of intensity that made her mouth go dry. He laced his fingers through hers and pulled her back against his chest.

"I was just trying to bully you into agreeing to a date with me," he whispered against her ear. "Right now is all about trying to impress you enough that you agree to a second one."

A second one.

Her eyes widened and a small smile teased her lips. She took a few breaths until she felt like she could tease him again.

"You trying to make an honest woman out of me or what?"

Shae regretted the teasing question as soon as it left her mouth. She'd always had a nasty habit of messing around and getting her feelings hurt. Kofi wanted to spend time with her before he went back to his life clear on the other side of the Atlantic Ocean. Why did she have to go make things weird by implying he wanted anything more than a good time?

"I don't know," he started and her heart sank somewhere to the bottom of her stomach. He brought his hand to her cheek and brushed his thumb across her face. "How many perfectly planned dates and expertly shot Instagram photos would it take for you to consider something like that?"

The left corner of his mouth turned up much in the same way it used to when he was trying hard to not tease her when they were growing up. Shae knew then that she hadn't been able to disguise the shock on her face.

"Stop messing around," she said eventually because she

couldn't think of an appropriate response to the question he'd thrown at her.

The small, half smile dropped from his face almost as if someone had wiped it off and Shae started worrying she'd inadvertently made him angry when he tipped her chin up so she could stare into those deep brown eyes that were filled with a bit of something she couldn't place. Not that she could devote much brainpower to trying to decipher anything with the way his erection pressed up against her stomach. Heat rushed to her cheeks.

"Get this straight, Shae Butter," he said. "I always mean what I say. But that will be a conversation for another day. Right now we're going to eat good food, drink strong cocktails and I'll get to watch your pretty ass laid out while the sun sets."

She released the breath caught in her throat as he leaned down and pulled her bottom lip between his teeth. "That sounds like a good time."

He grinned. "Come let me do my photography duties so I can get you in whatever bikini fits so comfortably in that small ass bag."

CHAPTER SEVENTEEN

Shae knew how to work the camera. Kofi was happy his photography talent, or lack thereof, didn't even factor into the equation. All that went into a perfect shot was Shae fixing the camera with those soulful eyes and flashing a smile. They took a few shots of her sitting around the open-air bar taking small sips of a Mai Tai before they moved to taking shots in front of the plunge pool right off the side of the bar. She positioned herself in the space between the pool and the daybed experimenting with a few poses while he snapped. The sun had become a ball of orange fire starting to make its slow descent through the clear sky. He pulled back and browsed through the photos, satisfied with the options. The kaleidoscope of colors between the daybed's blue cushions, the light blue water of the plunge pool, the contrasting blues of the ocean and the sky's orange hues provided a perfect backdrop for the real star. Yellow looked great on Shae and her skin practically glowed from the dying embers of sunlight reflected against it.

"I got some great shots," he said when he could finally drag his attention from the beautiful photos. "Let's head to dinner."

He reached for her and smiled when she placed her hand

into his as if she'd been doing it for her entire life. Her skin was soft and warm against his. Kofi felt his stomach tighten. She unleashed a different type of need burning deep in his belly. He'd searched hard for the perfect restaurant to plan their date and eventually called up Sheldon for tips. His best friend was excited when Kofi confessed he was trying to impress a woman he wanted to see where things could go with. If Sheldon was suspicious about his straight up refusal to give him details about this mystery woman, he didn't show it... too much. Kofi knew he would have to sit him down, sooner rather than later, if things would progress with Shae. But first he had to make sure Shae was down for something like that. She'd provided him with the perfect opening, but he'd backed down from it like a coward. Later would be better. He didn't want them to spend the rest of what could be a spectacular evening with awkwardness flowing between them. He squeezed her hand a little as the server led them down the wooden stairs to the restaurant's second pool. He'd asked for the best thing they had when he called to make reservations. The cheery woman on the phone suggested he booked the poolside sunset tasting menu. He heard a small gasp from Shae as she took in the table for two set up at the edge of the infinity pool. They strung fairy lights up around the space, offering a muted glow that Kofi knew would only become more beautiful once the place started getting dark.

"There are towels on the daybed," the server was saying as Shae took out her phone to snap a few photos. "We'll get started with dinner and then you can enjoy the pool."

He loved seeing the excitement on Shae's face as she mused about never being at the restaurant for dinner before.

"This is gorgeous," she gushed, her mouth curving into an even wider smile as she twisted in the chair to watch the last moments of the sunset.

"Yes, you are," he said.

"Stop it," she said, but the smile that made his heart beat faster was still plastered on her face. He'd been halfway through his comeback when the server reappeared with a bottle of Veuve Clicquot. She filled two glasses and told them she would return with the starter courses. Kofi raised his glass, "Let's toast."

"To what?" Shae asked. Skepticism laced her voice even though she raised her glass to his as she kept her eyes trained on him. He chuckled. Shae was horrified that time she visited Sheldon in Jamaica when they told her not making eye contact when toasting would cause bad sex for the rest of her life. Her reaction had been hilarious, as was Sheldon's when it slowly dawned on him that his little sister had a sex life to be concerned about.

"I can't believe you still take that seriously," he said.

She cocked her head to the side and laughed lightly as she pulled her lips through her teeth. He got even harder.

"I'd rather be safe than sorry," she said, even though he could hear the self-deprecation in her voice. "What are we toasting to?"

"New beginnings," he whispered, clinking their glasses together and keeping his gaze trained on her as he brought the glass to his lips. He hoped she could see every bit of the lust that burned through him reflected in his eyes.

"What new beginnings?" she asked.

"Hopefully," he started and then stalled for a few seconds before he found her gaze again. "Us."

CHAPTER EIGHTEEN

Hopefully us.

Shae's heart pounded so hard against her chest she could feel it in her ears. *Did he just say? Was he implying? Wait, what?*

"You don't have to look so horrified, Shae Butter. Stop gripping the glass so tight. I'm not washing any dishes to pay for it."

She laughed at the ridiculous statement before she realized she was really holding the glass with a death grip.

"You don't remember me very well if you think this is my horrified face," she said when she could finally make her mouth form words a few moments later. "This is my *trying to process what the fuck is going on* face."

Kofi began speaking but stopped when two servers returned with several plates. She bit her lips to tap down on the frustration that welled inside her at the interruption. Shae tried to focus on the plates of arugula and prosciutto salad, tuna tartare, guacamole, hummus and sticky pulled pork that were being arranged on the table, but her heart was lodged in her throat.

"There isn't a lot to process," Kofi said once the servers were out of earshot. "I like you."

The air around them crackled with something Shae couldn't

name but it felt potent, intense, and dangerous even. She squeezed her thighs together, trying to clamp down on both the intense physical and emotional reaction she was having. It didn't work, so she turned to the humor she often used to cloak her when she felt overwhelmed.

"I must got me some bomb ass pussy," she teased. "You caught feelings with swiftness."

"Bomb ass doesn't come close to describing your pussy," he shot back. Kofi's voice got huskier with each syllable. Her pussy throbbed like she knew she was being discussed and had something to add to the conversation. Shae couldn't meet Kofi's gaze even though she was the one who brought her pussy into the discussion.

"It has nothing to do with your pussy, though," he said. "I know you don't believe me but you didn't misread anything that night after Nocturnal. You've intrigued me for a while."

She turned his words over in her mind as she reached for her champagne.

"A while?"

"From the time you stepped out of Norman Manley International Airport that year you visited Sheldon for UWI's carnival."

Shae almost choked on the champagne she'd sipped. Her mind raced as she caught his eyes. "That was *years* ago."

Kofi nodded and reached for her hand, intertwining their fingers before he continued. "I remembered feeling so damn confused. I'd spent my entire life thinking about you as Sheldon's annoying little sister… oww."

He chuckled when he recovered from how hard she'd pinched his hand before she smiled at him like butter wouldn't melt in her mouth.

"You were annoying as hell though, Shae," Kofi insisted.

"Do you remember when you found Sheldon's condoms and tried to extort money from him to keep your mouth shut."

Shae giggled. Maybe he wasn't *too* wrong. She hadn't been the easiest little sister, but Sheldon gave just as good as he got.

"We're getting distracted," she said with a small smile. She still couldn't wrap her head around what Kofi was trying to tell her. She tried to focus on what he was saying as he started making circles on her wrists while he continued. "You walked out of the airport with the biggest, warmest smile on your face and it was like I was seeing you for the first time. I spent your entire visit trying to make sense of what was going on."

She sifted through her memories of that time but nothing stood out to her other than both Sheldon and Kofi being unusually short-tempered while one of their other roommates wouldn't leave her alone no matter how hard she tried to politely tell him she wasn't interested.

"I had no idea…"

Kofi chuckled. "Neither did I, but it was clear as hell by the time Nocturnal rolled around. I keep wondering what would have happened if I had given in and kissed you."

"We'd have had half drunk New Year's sex in your car," Shae said pointedly. "Instead, I went to my room and cried myself to sleep."

Kofi squeezed her hand slightly. "I'm sorry."

She tried to brush off the disappointment she felt, the disappointment that was also reflected in Kofi's eyes. He seemed to be acknowledging, as she was, that it was the embarrassment from the near kiss that led to her keeping her distance for so many years.

"Why didn't you?" she asked.

"You were Sheldon's little sister."

Shae raised an eyebrow. "I'm not sure if it's lost on you, but I'm *still* Sheldon's little sister. That hasn't changed."

He laughed but his voice was serious when he whispered, "But I have. When you started leaning in towards me that night all I could think about was how upset Sheldon would be if he found out we kissed."

"And now?"

"All I can think about is how upset I will be if I don't shoot my shot. I'm sorry for laying it so heavy on you. I promised myself I'd shut up about this and let us enjoy this time together."

"It's not overwhelming," Shae said. "Just unexpected. I thought all you were after was some fun."

Kofi smiled mischievously. "Oh, I'm after fun... *too*. I just want to know if we could explore this thing between us some more."

CHAPTER NINETEEN

I just want to know if we could explore this thing between us some more.

Shae used to think about how she'd react to Kofi confessing his feelings in quiet moments when she only had her thoughts for company. She didn't react in any of the ways she thought she might. She did not squeal or throw herself into his arms and kiss him sloppily. Instead, her mind raced. There were so many variables to account for. They didn't live in the same place, Sheldon could be a stubborn asshole when he wanted and what would a relationship between them truly look like?

"How much exploration can we do in less than two weeks?" she asked, pausing when the servers returned with more trays of food.

"It doesn't have to be just two weeks."

Shae had been piercing a piece of grilled garlic shrimp with her fork, but stopped when Kofi spoke as his implication washed over her. Her heart raced.

"Wait... are you saying I should come back to London with you?"

He shrugged, keeping his gaze fixed on Shae's widened eyes. "It depends."

"On what?"

His smile widened and just about took Shae's heart right with it. "How inclined you are to say yes."

KOFI WATCHED the emotions flitter across Shae's face and couldn't help smiling more widely. He was just as shocked as she was with the question that dropped out his mouth unrestrained by any filter or commonsense. But now he'd put it out there, Kofi didn't think it was as crazy at it sounded. Shae could do her job from anywhere she had a decent Internet connection. Hell, spending a few months in a new place might provide her with new, interesting content. Shae tipped her head backwards and laughed when he mentioned this. He wished he could take a snapshot to immortalize her... glass of wine in hand, curls falling into her face with the soft twinkle of the fairy lights behind her as she laughed in that unabashed manner that he loved so much.

"You really know how to sell an idea," she said. "A career opportunity, huh?"

She pushed back her chair and crossed the small distance between them, easing onto his lap and wrapping her hands around his neck. His body reacted immediately to her pressed up against him. He rubbed his hand up and down her exposed back before he brought his lips to hers.

"Everyone's going to have a lot to say," she said.

"I only care about what you have to say. Everyone else can go kick rocks."

Shae chuckled again. "Everyone else, huh? On a scale of

lose his shit to lose *all* his shit, how badly do you think Sheldon will react to our little exploration?"

Kofi hoped Shae didn't see the unease he felt reflected on his face. It didn't matter that Kofi knew he'd regret not taking a chance on seeing if things could blossom between him and Shae. He still didn't want to fall out with his best friend. A small part of him was still hoping that it wouldn't come to that, but Shae was right. Her brother was likely to react badly.

"He'll definitely lose all his shit," he said.

The small teasing smile dropped off of Shae's face and the mood around them changed to something more serious. "You sure you want to risk that?"

He cupped her face in his hands. "Do you remember that Christmas when I came home and Sheldon was too busy to pay any attention to me?"

She chuckled. "You mean the Christmas I realized childhood crushes die hard?"

"Yeah, that same one. The Christmas I realized we both had the same dorky obsession with James Bond films, you had a wicked sense of humor and your top lip curled whenever you were about to say something you knew you shouldn't. The Christmas I spent a shitload of time talking myself out of kissing you. I should've kissed you that time we watched *Die Another Day* when you threw popcorn at me and I tickled you until you cried. I definitely should've kissed you after Nocturnal because it was clear you wanted me to. I let my fear of Sheldon's opinion stop me. Right now, the only opinion that matters is yours. As I said before, everybody else can..."

"... kick rocks," she finished with another amused laugh.

"Precisely."

"Let me go change into my bikini and get into this pool," Shae said as she eased herself off him. "We need to make up for all the times you wanted to kiss me but didn't."

CHAPTER TWENTY

Shae pivoted on the balls of her feet and cast a glance over her shoulder so she could check out her reflection in restaurant's restroom mirror. She'd neatly folded her yellow jumpsuit before placing it in the clear plastic bag she'd had the presence of mind to bring.

"You looking good, girl," she laughed as she observed the bikini. She couldn't wait to see Kofi's reaction to the itty, bitty, yellow high cut bikini she'd chosen. Jada had given this bikini the highest rating during the try on haul. Her best friend raised the glass of wine she'd been drinking before letting out a raucous squeal and said, "This is the one. This is the soul snatching bikini right here."

Shae had done her best to show off the bikini for her viewers, but drew the line at turning around so they could see the back. YouTube would definitely demonetize her video if she'd done that. Kofi was about to see everything she'd had to hide. Shae shimmied her shoulders and smiled. She was feeling the fuck out of herself. All the heavy lifting she'd been doing in the gym was working for her. A little consistency made a big ass difference. Literally. Shae fluffed her hair one last time, took another quick glance in the mirror and made a mental note to outline a blog post about her fitness journey before she left the bathroom.

Kofi was standing around the bar laughing with the bartender while the young man prepared cocktails. Shae's breath caught in her throat as she stood still for a few seconds, just taking him in. Calling Kofi sexy as fuck was truly an understatement. It was an understatement while they were younger and it was an even greater understatement now. The years had treated Kofi the way most people probably prayed for. He'd not only grown into his looks but also his charm and overall swagger. The air around him vibrated with the confidence he exuded without appearing cocky. Shae was here for all of it. For all of him. She sighed happily as she finally made her way over to where he stood with butterflies fluttering to life in her stomach. Anticipation. After so many years, Shae didn't have to imagine how it would feel to step into Kofi's embrace. She didn't have to imagine how his hands would feel on her body. She didn't have to imagine how it felt to press her lips to his. She just could. And, damn, reality was so much better than anything she'd conjured up. Kofi and the bartender were still bantering about football fixtures when she stepped between his open legs and rest her cheek against his chest. He kissed the top of her head before moving seamlessly back into his conversation, as if sharing tender moments with her were the most natural and familiar thing in the world. He curled his fingers through hers as he laughed at the disparaging comment the bartender made about Kofi's favorite football team. Shae couldn't care less about whether Liverpool would win the Premiership league, but she loved listening to him speak. She loved the way the deep tone of his voice made the butterflies in her stomach flutter harder. She loved the way her pussy throbbed every time his chest vibrated with his laughter.

"Here's your Cosmopolitan," the bartender said, forcing her thoughts away from how ready she and her pussy were to have more of Kofi's undivided attention. She took the drink with a smile and eased herself from between Kofi's legs and started making her way back down to the infinity pool.

"Fuck."

The frustrated edge to Kofi's baritone pleased the hell out of Shae. She tossed a look over her shoulder and smiled widely when she saw that Kofi was already grabbing his cocktail from the bar and pushing himself to his feet. She put a bit more sway in her hips as she descended the steps.

Mission accomplished.

CHAPTER TWENTY-ONE

Kofi's heart slammed against his chest when Shae stepped out of the bathroom. It was immediately clear why her bikini fit so easily into the tiny ass clutch she brought with her. Damn. She sauntered from the bathroom towards the bar like she was gliding on air and Kofi felt his dick stir to life. The bartender, Devon, had been in the middle of a sentence when his words faltered. Kofi followed Devon's gaze right back to Shae and smiled. He didn't blame the man for being lost for words. Kofi couldn't even organize his thoughts. The bikini was a brighter shade of yellow than her jumpsuit and was even more magical against her deep brown skin. He struggled to pull his gaze away from the bikini top that left a flirty bit of under-boob on display but he couldn't. His gaze landed on her flat stomach, with a pineapple-shaped ring dangling from her belly button, and thick thighs as she continued making her way to him.

"Damn. That you?"

He turned his attention back to the man who stared at Shae with the kind of slack-jawed reverence Kofi related heavily to. *That you?* Kofi wasn't foolish enough to think he could say She was his. It didn't matter how much he hoped things would continue blossoming between them.

"I'm working on it," he said.

Devon chuckled as he poured the drink he was mixing into a shaker. He shook the concoction a few times before he turned his attention back to Kofi. "Better work hard."

"I am."

The shot of emotion deep in his chest when Shae stepped between his legs and cuddled herself into him wasn't a surprise. He was thankful Devon had returned their conversation to football so he had something else to focus on besides how good she felt wrapped up in his arms. He dropped a quick kiss on her forehead, knowing he needed to bring his conversation with Devon to an end so he could hold her the way he really wanted to. He'd slowly gotten used to her softness pressed up against him when Shae sauntered off with her Cosmopolitan in hand. That was when he truly saw what her bikini was made of.

"Fuck."

The word shot out of him before he could modulate the volume or tone. He could hear Devon chuckling beside him.

"Yeah, you better be trying hard," he said. "Cause... damn."

SHAE WAS ALREADY WADING into the infinity pool when he finally made it down the steps and into the small, private enclave they were using for the rest of the night. The effects of the fairy lights were more potent now that dusk began fading into nightfall. Someone had turned on the strategically placed lights around the pool and they cast their glow on the pitch-black water. Shae waded to the edge, taking small sips of her cocktail. He loved seeing her amongst the water and the lights looking so fucking ethereal, beautiful and perfect. He'd always look back at these moments with gratitude, no matter how things ended between them.

"This is so beautiful," she called over her shoulder. It was another one of those moments when he wished he had his phone out so he could take a snapshot of her immersed in the glowing water and looking over her shoulder with that broad, beckoning smile. He took one final chug of his cocktail before he placed the empty tumbler on a nearby table, pulled his shirt over his head and made his way into the pool.

"Yes, you are," he said.

She was still smiling when he was close enough to pull her into his arms. She nestled her cheek against his shoulder before she pulled back and wrapped her arms around his neck. His heart was no longer racing. It was thudding with the steadiest confirmation of the things he felt. He was halfway gone for Shae, and it was ridiculous to downplay it. Damn. Shae pressed her body against him so that her breasts flattened against his chest. Her soft, slick skin pressed against his body ignited his blood.

"You know I'm talking about the scenery."

Kofi cupped her ass as he hovered his lips over hers. "The scenery's aight," he teased. "But you? You're magical."

She smiled so widely her eyes became slits. He couldn't help but laugh before he finally allowed himself the pleasure of covering her mouth with his. She pressed into him as she opened her mouth so he could brush his tongue over hers. Kofi could easily lose himself in kissing Shae. He couldn't get enough of the way she dug her fingers into his neck as their tongues lashed together in a frantic, sensual dance. She tasted like citrus and the answer to all of his prayers. He hoped he could convince her to explore what could happen between them. His hands roved over her ass before he pushed her bikini bottoms to the side so he could slide a finger into her. She moaned against his mouth as he slid another finger into her pussy and started pumping them in and out of her. She was so soft. So hot. So tight. Kofi suddenly doubted the wisdom of touching her in the first place. Would he be able to stop? She clenched around his fingers and Kofi felt all his blood rush from his head to his dick. He brushed his thumb over her clit and rubbed in quick, firm circles until Shae's mewling moans got louder. Her body coiled tightly, the way it usually did when she was about to come. Kofi strummed her clit faster. He wanted nothing more than to watch and feel Shae fall apart in his arms. He kissed her cheek and dragged his lips along her jawline, chuckling when she titled her pelvis upwards as if she was trying to take his fingers as deep into her as they could go. He licked his lips and fought the base urge to pull his dick out of his swim shorts and thrust into her. God, he wanted to cocoon himself in her soft warmth.

"You're so fucking wet," he whispered into her ear. His voice was tight and rough, but Kofi didn't care that it was obvious he wanted her. She tipped her chin up as a small, mischievous smile rose on her face.

"Wanna feel?" she asked with a small chuckle cut short by a moan when he increased his finger's pressure against her clit.

"Don't make jokes like that when I'm barely hanging on to control as is. Keep playing and I'll be buried in your pussy before you can blink."

He continued squeezing her ass as he worked her over with his fingers, taking in each miniscule change in her expression as her body started succumbing to pleasure.

"I'm not joking," she said. She barely bit down another moan. Kofi didn't have time to fire off the teasing comment on his tongue before Shae was pushing her hands into his swim shorts and stroking his dick. His movements faltered when the delicious friction of her tight fist moving from his tip to his base in a steady, toe-curling rhythm washed over him.

"Kofi?" she whispered, her voice thick and husky with lust. He managed to pull his mind out of the fog to bring his eyes to hers. "Yes, babe?"

Her smile spelled trouble.

"I blinked."

CHAPTER TWENTY-TWO

Shae had no idea who this bold ass person inhabiting her body was or what they did to the Shae she'd grown accustomed to for the past thirty years. She couldn't believe she was propositioning Kofi to fuck her in public. Boldness, notwithstanding. Outrageousness, notwithstanding. Craziness, not withstanding. Shae couldn't think of a single thing she wanted more. Kofi's fingers were working her over splendidly, with just the right amount of teasing pressure and rhythmic strokes to send pleasure spiraling through her but it wasn't nearly enough. She wanted... no... she needed to feel Kofi's heaviness deep in her pussy. She wanted to feel her body stretch to accommodate him. She bit her lip so hard she tasted blood but it didn't dull her need for him. Not with his thumb stroking her clit in languid circles as she felt the first tremors of an orgasm erupting inside her. She came with a cry on her lips and stars behind her eyes. Shae breathed deeply, sure that her release would dull the ache deep in her core. She was wrong. Lust slammed into her as soon as her body stopped shaking with undulating pleasure. Everything else was just an appetizer, a stopgap, a placeholder for what her body really wanted: Kofi buried deep inside. He dragged his lips across her jaw and placed his forehead against hers. "You sure?"

Shae couldn't make her vocal cords work so she nodded.

"What if someone comes back down here?"

Panic shot through her, but it didn't have time to materialize into anything before lust chased it away. In that moment Shae didn't give a damn about someone possibly catching them in the act. She pushed Kofi's swim shorts down far enough for his dick to spring free and guided him to her entrance. She eased herself down on him, sighing with relief when his dick started sliding into her.

"We'll just have to make sure we give them a good show," she whispered, lifting herself and dropping back down. His hard thickness curved just enough that he hit her most sensitive spots with each thrust. Kofi's dick would be the death of her. But what a way to go!

"A good show, huh?" Kofi whispered, sucking her lips into his mouth before he pulled back and grinned. "Let's do it."

His voice, as deep as it was and as sexy as it was, hit her straight in the clit. Shae hadn't known it was possible, but she got wetter. She moaned into his neck when he grabbed her ass and lifted her up off him before he slammed into her. And then again. And then again. And then again. Her breasts were bouncing their way out of her bikini top, but Shae didn't give a damn. Shae couldn't give a damn about anything other than the way Kofi's dick felt inside her. Her pussy clenched hard around him as if she was afraid he'd take away her favorite plaything if she didn't hold him close. He palmed her ass, pulling her closer and positioning her so her clit rubbed against his pubic bone each time he thrust. She cried out his name. Cried out to God. Cried out to his dick. And then she sang praises to it, because how could she not worship a fuck like that? It was the kind of fuck that majored in the Arts of Good Dicking and earned straight A's. *Summa cum laude.*

"Damn it, Shae." Kofi murmured. "Why the fuck do you have to feel so good?"

He sounded like they were both walking the same edge and it was a toss up between who would fall off first. It didn't matter. They were playing a game where they both came out winners. Over and over again.

CHAPTER TWENTY-THREE

Kofi held heaven in his arms.

Heaven was Shae's soft, warm body pressed up against his as the cool ripples of pool water teased his skin.

Heaven was feeling Shae's pussy throb around him as she fell apart while she came.

Heaven was Shae's husky, soft moans against the crook of his neck as she trailed her shaking fingertips across his shoulders.

Heaven was the orgasm that rocked him straight from the top of his head to the tips of his toes. His stomach tightened and thighs clenched as he stopped fighting his release.

"Damn," he murmured into the top of Shae's head as the reality of what they'd just done slammed into him. He glanced around, half expecting to see someone standing around watching the show they'd put on. He chuckled. It would've been a hell of a show. He squeezed Shae's hips as he sought her mouth, kissing her with an intensity he hoped she could feel. She fit him so damn well. He'd been about to tell her this when he spotted movement out of the corner of his eye. A heavyset server was making her way down the stairs with what seemed like a tray of desserts and two fresh glasses of champagne. Shae flinched, so he rubbed slow circles against the small of her back.

"We're good," he whispered into her ear. "She won't suspect a thing."

His words seemed to relax her. She beamed at the woman as she approached the edge of the pool.

"How's your evening been?" the server asked.

"It's been euphoric," Shae said, flashing him a sly smile. He swore he fell a bit more for her in that moment. The server seemed none the wiser that as she spoke his dick was still buried in Shae and slowly getting hard again. She stuck around for a few more minutes before she headed back up the steps and Shae and Kofi collapsed into laughter.

"Euphoric, huh?" he teased.

She cupped his cheeks in her hands and stared at him for a few seconds before she said, "Beyond. I don't even know what I expected other than being excited that we would spend some time together. This... this was perfect, Kofi."

He brought his lips to hers and lingered, savoring how they felt against him.

"You're perfect."

Shae laughed—a deep belly laugh he could feel rumbling against his chest. "There's no need for flattery. You got my attention."

"Great. I think my dick has a few things he'd like to say."

Kofi thrust shallowly into her a few times before he hit her with a smooth, deep stroke. The moan caught in her throat was so deliciously arousing that he felt himself get even harder. He squeezed her hips as he settled into a slow, steady pace. It shouldn't feel so good. How did she feel so good? How the fuck could he burn so damn hot for her when he'd had her not ten minutes before. Hell, he hadn't even pulled his dick out before he was already raring to go again. Each brush of her supple, wet body against his and every soft, pleasure-filled cry that spilled from her mouth when he moved inside her, made him burn even hotter.

Kofi didn't want to fuck Shae in slow and steady strokes. He wanted to thrust into her hard, fast and deep with the unrestrained, ferocious need burning in the pit of his stomach. But he knew better than that. The last thing he wanted to do was draw attention to what they were doing in the pool, so he brought his lips back to Shae's and kissed away the urge the pummel into her. The orgasm was a slow burn, with her pussy clenching around him in small bursts even as she tried to push up closer to him while she dragged his earlobe through her teeth. Kofi moaned. He didn't grunt. He didn't growl. He didn't groan. He straight up moaned. And Kofi didn't give a damn. He didn't give a damn about how his toes curled either. Her pussy had the type of grip that had dancehall songs dedicated to it.

"Jesus Christ," he murmured, hooking his hand under her knees so he could open her wider for him. Shae squeezed her eyes shut and nuzzled into his neck as her moans got louder and her pussy clenched tighter. He held out for as long as he could, but soon his body shook and mind spun as Shae brought her mouth roughly to his while they came together.

CHAPTER TWENTY-FOUR

Shae awoke to the flutter of fingers trailing a light path down her stomach. She wriggled closer to the solid warmth pressed against her back.

"Good morning, sleepyhead," Kofi whispered into her ear. A shiver shot down her spine as she turned in bed so she could face him. He looked ridiculously handsome, ridiculously sexy and ridiculously awake, considering they hadn't done much sleeping the night before. She brushed her finger across a portion of Kofi's beard that she knew for sure was still wet with her juices from where she gushed against his face barely an hour ago.

"Why are you so chirpy for someone who hasn't slept?" she asked and then giggled when he said in a deadpan voice. "Your pussy is revitalizing."

Shae checked her Fitbit and grimaced when she realized it was pushing eight. She had a shitload of things she needed to do for work but wanted nothing more than to snuggle back into Kofi and drift off into the satisfied slumber only a woman who'd had an orgasm-filled night could achieve.

"Time to kick me out?" Kofi teased. His hand snaked around her waist and came to rest on her ass.

"Yes," she said but softened it by leaning in for a short, sweet kiss. "But I'll at least make you breakfast before you leave."

"You don't have to do that. I'm sure the hotel already put out the buffet."

Shae wished he would stop rubbing and squeezing her ass. It was awakening desires that should have been exorcized the night before. It took nearly another fifteen minutes of fooling around before Kofi finally stopped stroking Shae's pussy, fondling her breasts and running his lips across her exposed to skin.

Shae swung her feet over the side of the bed before she glanced at Kofi with a small, shy smile. "Maybe we can make it quick?"

He was on her before she could take a breath, pinning her against the bed with his erection pressed against her leg.

"Thank God," he breathed against her collarbone. "I was about to beg."

Shae laughed. "Damn. I shoulda waited."

His smile was broad and teasing and... beautiful. She ran her finger across his cheek before tilting her chin so she could brush her lips against his. She gasped when she felt the head of his dick slowly sliding against her pussy. Shae didn't think she would ever get tired of the explosive sensation that always rocked her body when he first slid into her. She wrapped her legs around his waist, pressing her heels into his ass, urging his quick, powerful strokes as she dragged her fingers down his back. He nuzzled his head in the crook of her neck... sucking on, licking, and gently grazing her skin as he pushed her closer and closer to an orgasm every time he slammed his dick into her.

Her buttocks clenched. Her pussy clenched. Her clit throbbed.

And then her body crumbled under the force of the pleasure shooting through her. Shae wasn't inexperienced. She'd had a lot of good sex. She'd had a lot of great sex. She'd even had sex that just about blew her mind. But she'd never had sex like this. She'd never come like this. Her pussy seemed like it was about to push Kofi's dick out with its forceful spasms. It didn't take long before Kofi's body followed. He called her name and muttered curses as he pressed open-mouthed kisses all over her face and lips while he came. Shae couldn't stop grinning when she finally extricated herself from Kofi's limbs and headed to the bathroom to clean up. The sluggish tiredness she'd been feeling had all but disappeared. Who would've thought having Kofi fuck her awake would be more potent than any double espresso she'd ever had?

CHAPTER TWENTY-FIVE

His mind wouldn't turn off or slow down the erotic slideshow starring Shae that played on a loop. The slideshow would provide ample material for when he was ready to jack off to memories of Shae, but it wasn't particularly helpful now he was sitting across from her very inquisitive brother.

"You good?" Sheldon asked for the fifth time in half of an hour. "You keep disappearing somewhere."

Between your sister's thighs, Kofi thought. He flashed his best friend a wry smile instead.

"I'm good. Just going over the strategy I'm going to use to kick your ass later."

Sheldon laughed. "You've never beat me in basketball. Not even once."

"There's a first time for everything," Kofi teased. "Come get your ass whopped."

He and Sheldon met up on the public basketball court near where they lived growing up for a game of one on one. Sheldon had jokingly asked him if he'd come back to Antigua for his engagement party or if it was just an excuse to chase after this mystery woman Kofi was being tightlipped about. Kofi couldn't think of a good way to answer the question but it turned out he didn't have to. Sheldon easily switched the conversation to listing a bunch of things they could do once they finished with the game. They settled on meeting up with a few of their friends for drinks. Sheldon's teasing comment stayed on Kofi's mind long after the conversation shifted. He hadn't come up with a good plan to ease Sheldon into what was going on between him and Shae. He wasn't sure there *was* a good way to ease Sheldon into what was going on between him and Shae. The clock continued ticking by. He only had ten days left before he returned to London, and he would try everything in his power to make sure Shae came back with him. The first step in doing that was sorting out the Sheldon situation and whatever fallout came from it. Yet, the words stuck to his throat whenever he thought of bringing it up. Kofi tried to put the worry from his mind and focus on enjoying playing basketball with Sheldon.

He lost, just as Sheldon predicted, but it was fun running up and down the court, jostling and talking shit to each other throughout the game.

"Maybe you'll win next time," Sheldon teased, dribbling the ball for a few more seconds before he effortlessly landed a shot from behind the perimeter.

"Unlikely," Kofi laughed. "What time are we planning to meet at Quentin's place?"

Sheldon checked his watch. "Around four. Why? Trying to see if you have enough time to sneak by your lady love?"

He was but he wasn't going to tell Sheldon that. It would only lead to more questions about who she was. So he lied.

"My mother called the other day," he said. "Been wondering if I should drop by and play nice. I don't think I'll hear the end of it if I left without showing my face."

"You need to do more than drop by your mother," Sheldon muttered. "You need to talk to that woman."

"To what end?" Kofi asked. He kept check of the irritation in his voice. It didn't make any sense for him to get irritated with Sheldon for following him straight down the rabbit hole he'd opened up to divert attention away from his love life.

"Our parents are getting older. You don't want to look back a few years from now and realize you let childhood angst propel you to act in ways you regret."

Sheldon cut off the response that burned Kofi's throat. "I'm not downplaying how abandoned she made you feel so don't lay into me. I'm not even saying you need to have a relationship but you need to talk to her. Let her know how her actions affected you and then move from there."

Kofi turned over Sheldon's suggestion in his mind before he decided he didn't have the time or emotional reserve to deal with it at that moment.

"I'll see you at Quentin's," Kofi said, patting Sheldon on his shoulder. "I might be a little late."

Sheldon shook his head. "I know you were just trying to distract me but I let it slide cause you needed to hear what I had to say. Don't think I won't eventually make you tell me whose pussy you've been sniffing around."

Kofi smiled tightly. That was exactly what he was afraid of.

CHAPTER TWENTY-SIX

"Shae! In public," Jada yelled. "In the people's bourgeois, expensive ass pool. You realize the next people to use that pool will be swimming around in your pussy juices, right?"

Shae crinkled her nose. "Jada stop being nasty."

Jada placed her hand to her chest. "Me? Being nasty? *Me?* This is coming from you... the one who just got the shit fucked out of her in Sheer Rock's plunge pool? I should send them an anonymous request the drain the damn thing."

"You are doing the most," Shae laughed. "I shouldn't have told you anything."

Jada rolled her eyes at the weak threat. Shae told Jada everything. Her best friend had barely stepped into the house before she launched into a detailed retelling of her night with Kofi. She'd expected Jada to focus on Kofi actually liking her, wanting to see where things could go and inviting her back to London. But Jada couldn't get past the sex in the pool bit. Shae's cheeks still went hot just thinking about it.

"Of course I'm doing the most. I'm salty. You're getting your pussy catered to. Meanwhile, I can't even sing WAP. I sing DAP... ain't nothing over here but my dry ass pussy."

Shae laughed so hard she spat out the iced coffee she was drinking. Droplets landed on the screen of her iMac.

"Jada," she groaned. "I asked you to come over to do your voiceover for the birthday party decoration vlog, not to kill me."

Jada shrugged. "You won't stop me from speaking my truth."

"Whatever, Jada."

"Don't get sassy now that you got yourself a little boyfriend. I will not tolerate the disrespect."

"Jada..." Shae stopped, shook her head and chuckled. "You know what. You're a lost cause."

Jada dropped her head on Shae's shoulder and pulled her into a side hug. "But you love me."

"More than anything," Shae admitted. "But please can we get to work?"

It took a few more minutes before they finally settled down and started working on the voiceovers to explain certain things about Jada and Regina's set up for Shae's birthday party. Shae knew quite a bit of her followers were looking forward to the Jada centric vlog. They always showed love to her when she popped up in Shae's weekly vlogs, and the haul video she featured on was doing exceptionally well. Jada didn't bring Kofi back up until they took a break from editing.

"Are you going to take him up on his offer?"

Shae sighed as she sank further into her office chair. "I want to. I really do."

"So the answer should be easy then."

Shae shook her head. "I wish. I don't think Kofi seriously considered how much Sheldon'll hate this."

Jada rolled her eyes. "I think you're giving Sheldon's opinion way too much importance."

"He's his best friend. I don't want Kofi to risk twenty-seven years worth of friendship just to explore something that might not even go anywhere."

"If Sheldon is willing to throw away twenty-seven years worth of friendship over who Kofi wants to stick his dick into, then the friendship was probably not worth it."

Shae understood where Jada was coming from but she wasn't sure she agreed. She'd seen Kofi and Sheldon's friendship in practice and it was a beautiful thing. They moved more like brothers than best friends but no matter how hard Sheldon wanted to believe it, Kofi was not *her* brother.

"I could understand if Kofi was going after one of his serious exes or something," Jada continued. "But, you? I can't even wrap my head around what his problem is. Did I ever tell you he made a pass at me?"

It was Shae's turn to roll her eyes. "No, Jada. It's not like you mention it twice per day or anything. You know it's not the same thing, right? Kofi and Sheldon have been friends forever. We'd only just started becoming friends when that happened."

"Once again, you won't stop me from speaking my truth."

Jada's antics were a great ass distraction, but it didn't stop the small knot of fear in the pit of her stomach. Shae hated conflict. She definitely didn't want to cause any trouble between Sheldon and Kofi. She thought about how easy it was to be in Kofi's company. Then she thought of how much her body craved his touch. Her pussy responded to him like he owned it. She thought about having to give him up before they truly got started and realized it didn't sit well with her soul. She hoped Sheldon could get his ass together because Shae didn't think she had it in her to walk away.

"I was thinking about a series called *A Caribbean Girl Takes London* for YouTube and the blog. How does that sound?"

Jada smiled brightly. "It sounds like you've made the right decision."

CHAPTER TWENTY-SEVEN

Kofi had every intention of surprising Shae with lunch and some dick before he got ready to head to Quentin's house to meet up with the guys. He wasn't sure when he knew he would deviate from the plan, but he was regretting the hell out of it as he sat in his rental and observed the house he grew up in. Damn Sheldon for getting in his head. He didn't call his mother to tell her he was coming and he wondered if popping up on her was a good idea. He almost used that as an excuse to leave but as soon as he started the car, he turned it off again. He'd already come this far. It made little sense backing down now.

His mother's eyes widened and her mouth parted when she opened the front door and saw him standing on the other side. She didn't attempt to hug him, but Kofi couldn't blame her for that. She probably had no idea how he would react if she tried. He had no idea how he would react if she tried.

"Hi Deborah," he said once he realized she wouldn't break the ice. He'd stopped calling her mom the moment he turned eighteen. Initially she challenged it, immediately appreciating the intended disrespect. Eventually, she realized it was easier to stop fighting him on it. His mother often took the easiest way out.

"I didn't expect to see you."

"I know," he said. He shifted his weight from one foot to the other. He was thirty-two years old but standing in front of his mother taking in her dark skin and elegant features, he felt like a child again. A fresh stab of pain resurfaced and he was once again annoyed he allowed Sheldon to get in his head. Another few seconds passed before Deborah got over the shock of seeing him and stepped aside so he could enter the house. The house was different from the last time he'd visited four years ago. There was new furniture and a different shade of paint on the walls. The Christmas lunch he'd shared with his mother and her husband was awkward as hell but still not nearly as painful as many dinners he'd shared with them in the past.

"Is he in?"

His mother shook her head. "He's in Guyana visiting family."

Kofi didn't react to the extra bit of information she offered about his stepfather. He didn't really care.

"Do you want some juice? I made some tamarind drink the other day. I know you used to like it."

Her voice sounded stiff and formal, but Kofi recognized something lingering under it. She was nervous. He shoved his hands into the pockets of his sweats just to find something to do with them before he told her he would like a glass. She wasn't wrong. He loved the sweet, tart drink as a child and he still loved it now. He couldn't remember the last time he'd had it.

"Have a seat," she said, gesturing to the couch. "I'll be right back."

He took a seat on the far end of the chocolate brown couch but was sitting for barely ten seconds before he was on his feet again. He paced the length of the living room as he acknowledged his own nerves. Was he really going to talk to his mother about all the things from his childhood he still resented her for? What difference would it make now? He was a grown ass man. But he supposed Sheldon was right. Maybe he would feel better just getting things out in the open. He'd often made snide comments but they usually stopped short. He never mentioned the hurt, the raw pain he still felt. He'd never looked his mother in her eyes and told her how often he felt like she chose her husband, who hated him, over her own son. He never told her he felt abandoned, unprotected and that was why he used to spend as much time out of the house as he could. She returned a few minutes later with a large glass of tamarind juice and ice and a smaller glass of water. He noticed her hands shook slightly when she handed him the juice.

"Thanks," he said. He took a sip of the juice to stall before he said. "I think we need to talk."

His mother nodded sharply, taking a small sip of her water. "I think it's overdue."

Kofi sat down and his mother joined him.

"I know I've made myself scarce over the last couple years. It must have been a shock to you when I left for London to do my Masters and didn't come back."

"I thought you were trying to find the best opportunities," she said. "It wasn't until later I realized you were just trying to get away from me."

His heart slammed against his chest when he heard the resignation in her voice. She spoke with quiet conviction, but what she was saying wasn't true. Not entirely.

"It's never been you I was trying to get away from and you must know that by now. You have to."

She was silent. She just pressed her lips together, held her jaw tight, straightened her back and looked past him. The seconds ticked by and disappointment rushed through Kofi. This really was a waste of time. He placed his near empty glass of tamarind juice on the side table and pushed himself to his feet.

"I'm going to go."

Deborah rose with him. "Just say what you came here to say, Kofi. I know you came to call me a shit mother and try to justify why you never visit or call. I'm not sure what you expected me to do because you didn't get along with my husband."

Kofi's eyes widened. "Did not get along with? Is that how you really see it? I was a child. That man despised that you came with *baggage* and he made sure I never forgot it."

His mother sucked her teeth. "He never raised his hands to you."

"Because abuse is always physical?" Kofi shot back, barely keeping check of the anger in his voice. "I can't believe you're really standing here pretending that Gerald didn't make my childhood a living hell..."

"He did right by you. Who put you through University?"

"My scholarship."

"Your scholarship didn't feed you for those three years you were in Jamaica."

Kofi shook his head. Another surge of annoyance rushed through him. He shouldn't have allowed Sheldon to get in his head.

"It was nice seeing you," he said stiffly before he started for the door.

"We did right by you," his mother shouted after him, her voice almost shrill. Kofi's shoulders sagged but he didn't look back. He was suddenly exhausted and not feeling up to hanging out with five rowdy guys without a single chill bone between them. He shot Sheldon a quick message telling him he had to skip on meeting at Quentin's and then turned off his phone so he didn't have to face the inevitable inquisition. Then he headed to the only place he wanted to be.

CHAPTER TWENTY-EIGHT

Shae leaned over her tub and checked the water's temperature. She'd had a productive, but exhausting day and was looking forward to spending a few hours soaking in the tub that had been the selling point of the house before turning in for the night. She dropped a few drops of lavender and peppermint essential oils into the warm water and removed her robe. She was about to step into the tub when she heard a few loud raps. She paused for a while but bundled herself back up in her robe and padded to the front door when the knocks sounded again. Her lips parted when she saw Kofi standing at the door when she swung it open. She was about to tease him about not being able to stay away from her when she took a good look at him and her stomach plummeted.

"What's wrong? Did Sheldon flip out when you told him?"

The questions came out in one long, anxious breath. Shae was even more confused when Kofi assured her that Sheldon had nothing to do with his current mood. She stepped aside and allowed him into the house, turning and pulling him into a tight hug.

"Tell me what you need," she whispered. He dragged his

gaze over her as if he was noticing what she was wearing for the first time.

"Did I interrupt your bath?"

"I was just getting in. Had a bunch of relaxing essential oils going." She played with the hem of his white shirt before starting to pull it over his head.

"I think you should join me while we talk about whatever has you looking so damned sad."

He sighed. "I think it's a conversation better paired with hard liquor."

Shae's mind raced. What could have happened in the few hours they hadn't been texting back and forth that was so bad? She tried to keep her face neutral despite the intense worry surging through her.

"I can offer you a relaxing bath, liquor and some pussy," she said with a small smile. "In that order."

The tension in her stomach loosened a bit when he smiled. "That sounds good."

SHAE TRIED to resist the urge to ask Kofi to tell her what was going on as she led him to the bathroom. She sat at the edge of the tub while he undressed before climbing in.

"I thought you said the water was warm," he exclaimed. "This is hot. Really hot."

Shae chuckled. "Because it *is* warm. Stop overreacting."

He muttered something about women's skin being made to withstand the flames of hell and a surprisingly vicious wave of jealousy rose in Shae.

"You be bathing with a lot of women?" she asked, dropping the robe and crawling right on top of him in the tub. He flashed her that adorable as hell smile and shook his head while he brought his hands to cup her ass. "I'm not allowing you to tie me up with that."

Shae chuckled. She let the irrational jealousy to flow out of her. Kofi was here with her when he could have been anywhere else if he wanted to be. She kissed him softly and slowly before she deepened the kiss, running her tongue along the insides of his mouth, barely swallowing a moan of satisfaction when she heard him groan in his throat. He traced his fingertips along her spine and she pushed herself closer to him, eager to feel as much of his body as she could. Desire didn't run through her like wildfire this time. It moved like molasses, slowly but so potent and thick she found it hard to breathe. Reality crashed over her when she felt his erection throb against the inside of her legs. She reluctantly broke the kiss, tugging at his bottom lip as she slowly moved her mouth away.

"We should talk," she suggested. "I want to know what's wrong with you."

One of Kofi's hands returned to her ass while the other slid between their bodies and found the sweet spot between her legs. She moaned when he pressed her clit between his thumb and index finger and rubbed it lightly. So much for good intentions. She tried to ease him into conversation again but he silenced her by crashing his lips against hers. Her chest heaved when he finally pulled away.

"Well talk," he whispered gruffly against her cheek. "But right now I just want to enjoy you."

Shae brought her lips roughly back to his. If he wanted distraction, she'd give him distraction. She rocked her hips forward so her pussy brushed against his dick, sliding it between her already slippery folds and moaning loudly when Kofi squeezed her ass even tighter.

"Lemme have you, Shae Butter," he groaned. Shae didn't

need to be told twice. She slid up his dick one more time before she slid her hand down his stomach and lifted herself off him so she could hold his dick. She stroked him for a short while before she positioned him at her entrance and sank down on him. Shae grabbed his shoulder as she rolled her hips with his thick, heavy dick cocooned snuggly inside her throbbing pussy. God, he felt good. She couldn't get enough. Shae continued rolling her hips as Kofi grabbed her ass and pulled her so close into him that no space remained between them. He massaged her ass cheeks even as her movements became more frantic, sliding a finger down her ass crack and then up again before he paused slowly, hovering as if he was waiting for her...

"Yes please," she breathed and grunted when she felt a thick finger slide inside. Her movements faltered as she rode the twin peaks of pleasure but Kofi barely missed a beat, jerking his own hips forward, slamming into her until beads of lights pricked behind her eyes. The water sloshed over the sides of the tub but Shae couldn't find it in herself to care that she would have to clean it up later. Not when Kofi was filling her up in the best ways possible. The thick, silky length of his dick hitting against her pleasure spots, his finger making circular motions in her ass until she clenched against him, his tongue exploring hers in languid strokes as if he was trying to paint a masterpiece in her mouth. All while her body pressed so tightly into him that her hardened nipples brushed against his chest each time he moved. Every nerve ending in her body buzzed. Fuck drugs. Shae could get high on Kofi's dick any day.

"I should be the one helping you," she murmured. She pulled her lips away from his. "I feel like I'm getting the better end of the deal."

Kofi chuckled but he didn't let up on his sweet, sensual strokes. Her body was so overwhelmed by the delicious pleasure starting to unfurl in her stomach that tears leaked from her eyes as Kofi crashed his mouth over hers. When he pulled away, he smiled at her and her heart flip-flopped.

"You're just what I need," he murmured. His lips roved over her mouth more gently when they found hers again. Shae's heart thumped against her chest but she couldn't spend any time analyzing the tenderness she swore she heard in his voice. Not when her body was combusting with each breathtaking stroke. Her pussy clenched rapidly around his dick as the orgasm roared to life inside her.

"Come for me, Shae Butter," Kofi groaned. "Come all over my dick."

Shae swallowed the moan in her throat, seeking Kofi's mouth as she obeyed his command.

CHAPTER TWENTY-NINE

It took forever before Kofi regained control of his limbs. Shae came more violently than he'd ever seen her come before and he followed behind her almost immediately. He was happy he came to Shae when his emotions were running high. It wasn't just because of the sex either, even though he wondered if Shae's pussy was laced with cocaine. It was her presence. Just seeing her come to the door with her fluffy, white robe pulled around her and twist-outs in disarray, shot a ray of light through the darkness that was surging through him. *She* was a ray of light. It didn't matter how things turned out between them, Kofi was happy he'd put all his cards on the table. He was happy he was able to experience her, fully experience her, even if it was just for a short time. Shae was butt ass naked with her smooth brown skin glistening with the last remnants of the bath water, sifting through her liquor cabinet to find what she said would be the perfect rum for him to drink while he poured out his soul to her. He actually looked forward to working through his feelings with Shae. He looked forward to her perspective, her advice and her comfort. If only his body would cooperate. He pulled his gaze away from the way her glistening pussy looked as she bent over to grab a bottle.

Focus. Kofi chuckled as his gaze went straight back to Shae's body. Cocaine pussy, indeed.

"Aha!"

Shae's victorious laughter sounded in the air as she turned around holding a rum with a black label and colorful wording in the air.

"Bambarra?"

She nodded and began making her way to where he sat around the kitchen table with two ice-filled tumblers and the bottle of rum. Her full breasts jiggled as she walked and Kofi groaned.

"Me and Jada spent a week in Turks and Caicos early last year. This is their local rum. I'm in love with it."

She sat opposite Kofi, poured two fingers of rum and pushed a tumbler in his direction. He sipped at it and was immediately impressed by the complexity of flavors that hit his tongue. He took a bigger sip and then a gulp.

"You're not wrong."

Shae smiled. "I've been drinking it sparingly, but I'm willing to drain this bottle for you."

His throat constricted as he reached over and covered her hand with his.

"Why did I wait so long to tell you how I felt?" he asked. It was during moments like this Kofi wished, again, that he'd had to balls to act on his feelings for her that Christmas.

"It doesn't matter," she said. "Maybe the Universe just wasn't ready for us yet."

She topped up his glass before she turned concerned eyes on him. "What's going on, Kofi?"

"I went to see my mother today," he said as if it explained

everything, and from the way Shae's forehead crinkled and eyes filled with sympathy, perhaps he had.

"I'm sorry," she whispered. "I take it things didn't go well."

He chuckled but there was only bitterness there. "It went worse."

He took a large sip of the rum before he launched into an often halting run down of Sheldon's speech and his eventual visit to his mother.

"She all but called me ungrateful and pointed out Gerald never hit me. This is the man who would tell me my mother should've aborted me because I ruined her life so often that I'd started believing it."

"I don't understand how anyone could be so cruel to a child."

Kofi swirled the rum around his glass, staring into the amber liquid as if it contained all the answers of the Universe. Not that he needed to look anywhere for the answer to Shae's question. He knew the answer. He'd known the answer as soon as he was old enough to put things together. Gerald and his mother had been high school sweethearts before the man called time on the relationship. The way people around the village told it, Gerald had ripped out, broken and pissed on Deborah's heart. She pined for him but eventually moved on to Kofi's father, a man he'd never met. Their relationship was brief and his father left Deborah's life and Antigua just as swiftly as he had come into it. By the time Gerald realized he wanted to be with Deborah she had a five-year-old in tow; a five-year-old who probably continuously reminded him that his wife once loved and created life with another man. It didn't help that Deborah and Gerald could not conceive despite years of trying. Maybe *that* was what caused the bitterness that led his stepfather to treat him like he was something nasty he picked up under his shoe. His mother often pretended she didn't hear the comments or see the fear in Kofi's eyes whenever he had to be alone with her husband. It had been over twenty-five years and Kofi still couldn't understand if she was just that naïve or if she simply didn't want to lose the man she'd once lost again. Whatever it was, home was unbearable for Kofi and he sought solace in the love filled Abbott household. He couldn't think about what his childhood would have been like if he and Sheldon hadn't been best friends. He *didn't* want to think about what his childhood could have been like. He didn't share with Sheldon what was going on until they were in their early teens but his best friend confessed he always suspected something was wrong at home and that was why he kept inviting him to sleepovers as often as he could get away with it. Kofi rarely had to ask to escape his house because Sheldon was always giving him excuses to. Guilt gnawed at his stomach. Was this how he was repaying his friend's loyalty? By fucking with the one person he'd repeatedly told him he didn't want him to?

"Don't feel guilty for distancing yourself from your mother if you believe it's best for you," Shae was saying. "It doesn't matter what she says. She knows she didn't show up for you when you needed her."

He tried to refocus his attention on the conversation but guilt became a tourniquet around his throat.

"I guess I'll always have a complicated relationship with my mother," he admitted. "I was open to seeing if we could hash things out today but as soon as we started talking I knew it wouldn't happen. I look at the relationship you guys have with your parents and sometimes I'm jealous but maybe that was just not in the cards for me. I've got to come to peace with that."

"Have you ever thought about therapy?"

Kofi had toyed with the idea of therapy on and off throughout the years but he never seemed to be able to make himself go. He explained this to Shae and she smiled at him.

"I'll give you that push you need when I come to London with you. I think therapy could do wonders..."

Her voice trailed off as the open, happy expression on her face faded into something he hated to see. Kofi sighed, knowing his worries must have shown on his face.

She swallowed, pressing her mouth into a tight line before she said, "I guess you changed your mind."

He shook his head. "I haven't. I still want to see where this goes..."

"But..."

"Talking about how much Sheldon helped me through my crappy ass childhood makes me realize I might not be as okay with him being pissed enough to end our friendship as I convinced myself."

Kofi wished he could take the words back as soon as they were out of his mouth. Not because they weren't true, but because he hated to see the hurt that flashed across Shae's face. He hated knowing he'd put it there. Kofi felt like shit. He should've left things alone. But he'd been so damn sure he was prepared to ride out the consequences. He'd met her initial hesitance with certainty only to express doubts once she'd gotten used to the idea.

"I'm sorry," he said. His fingers itched to reach for her but he resisted the urge, not knowing if she'd welcome his touch.

"It's okay," Shae replied in a brittle tone.

"You don't have to say that to make me feel better," Kofi said.

She shrugged. "I'm not. The thing is... I understand. I'm just not happy that this is something we need to be thinking about in the first place. I enjoy being around you and I feel like we could have something great. I don't want to miss out on that because Sheldon is an ass."

Kofi chuckled. "Preaching to the choir."

He reached out and touched her then, placing his palm to her cheek and sighing when she turned into his touch and kissed his wrist. The emotion flooding him was so deep and so intense that he had to close his eyes to catch his bearings.

"I'll talk to Sheldon," he said eventually. "I'll talk to him and see where he stands."

Shae shook her head. "You have over a week left. Can't we just… enjoy each other for that time? Maybe you can talk to him nearing the end?"

Shae's suggestion had dangerous written all over it. It wasn't wise to spend more time with her, possibly falling deeper for her and adjusting to having her in his life only for Sheldon to throw a wrench in things once he talked to him. It was risky as hell but he wanted it so badly his heart ached. So, despite knowing better, Kofi linked his fingers through Shae's and kissed her forehead. "You've got yourself a deal."

CHAPTER THIRTY

"What crawled up your ass and died there?"

Shae knew any response she'd have for Sheldon would be out of pocket, so she kept her head down and continued pushing her food from side to side on her plate. She never missed Sunday dinner at her parents' house. Her mother always cooked a huge spread so she had an excuse to leave with a few containers to last her a couple days of the next week. It was a win/win scenario all around, except she hadn't been prepared to step into her parents' expansive kitchen to find Sheldon sitting around the kitchen island holding a glass of brown liquor loosely in his hand. She and Sheldon always had a close, if not teasing and irreverent, relationship and Shae always looked forward to seeing her brother. The irritation that shot straight through her when Sheldon slid off the bar stool and walked over to her with his arms extended for a hug was foreign but not entirely unexpected. Five days had passed since Kofi had shown up to her house seeking comfort after the encounter with his mother and Shae alternated between irritation and fury. She loved her brother. Truly. Deeply. But every time she looked up from her plate and saw him smiling or making a joke with their parents, she wanted to throttle him. During all those years she pined for Kofi, she never imagined that Sheldon... *Sheldon*... might be the thing stopping them from getting together. She hadn't just been trying to pacify Kofi when she said she understood why he felt like he was betraying his best friend but Jada was right. This wasn't high school. Sheldon was a grown ass man and it wasn't as if Kofi was trying to get with Kara. She spent most of the lead up to dinner while her father watched cricket and their mother moved around the kitchen, wanting to blurt out to Sheldon that she'd been fucking his best friend. Thankfully reason prevailed, just barely, because she didn't think this was a fall out she wanted to have in front of her parents while they dug into their potato salad. Her mother loved excitement, from whatever source, but she doubted her father would be as easygoing. She'd also break her promise to Kofi and Shae didn't want to do that. They'd agreed to spend a few more days in their little bubble before Kofi had the conversation with Sheldon. Her annoyance faded slightly as she thought out the time she spent with Kofi. The past five days were all at once made from the stardust of her wildest dreams and poignantly and perfectly real. Her bond with Kofi felt more solid than anything she'd ever experienced and she realized it wasn't just the remnants of her childhood crush. She was completely enamored with grown up Kofi. She was enamored with his quirky sense of humor, his thoughtfulness and the way her soul just seemed to be able to rest easy in his presence. It was in the way his interest in her job never seemed feigned or forced. Two nights ago, before their Netflix and chill date turned into sweaty entangled limbs, Kofi watched her birthday vlog nearly ten times pointing out where he thought she could tidy up transitions. Then, he made a big production about being the first person to watch the vlog when it went live in the morning. Her cheeks strained against the broad grin that wanted to break free just thinking about it. That they had a lot of things in common wasn't a surprise. She'd realized that when they spent time together during that Christmas. She just never expected those commonalities to result in them being curled on her couch powering through Dr. Who episodes while eating cold pizza. Nor did she expect the rush of tenderness she felt when she kicked his ass in Call of Duty for the fifth time and he'd taken to trying to distract her with a barrage of kisses which eventually led to her straddling him and fucking him right there on the living room floor.

"Seriously Shae. What the hell is up with you?"

Sheldon's concern tinged voice pulled her from the memories that made her cheeks flush. Annoyance stabbed through her again when she thought about how much rested on how he reacted. She started saying something snide when her smart watch vibrated with an incoming message. She skimmed it before pushing her chair back and placing noisy kisses on her parents' cheeks.

"I've got a bunch of videos to edit," she lied. "Save some leftovers for me mommy, cause you know I'll be back to collect. Don't allow the bottomless pit to take it all."

She flashed Sheldon what she hoped was a genuine smile before she hustled herself out of the house. She waited until she'd already started her car and was backing out of the driveway before she made the call.

"You're early," she accused as soon as Kofi answered his phone. He chuckled and her body shivered at the sound.

"I wasn't trying to rush you, Shae Butter. I just wanted you to know I let myself in."

"As if I was going to spend more time trying to stop myself from slapping your boy when I knew you were probably stealing my chocolates and curled up in my bed."

His gruff laughter made her smile, and then she went warm inside when he said, "Oh so you know me *know me* then."

"I'll be there soon," she said. "Save at least one chocolate for me."

"Anything for my girl."

Her heart slammed against his chest. He said it with so much certainty that she almost wanted to believe that they'd find a way to be together no matter the outcome with Sheldon. She brushed her longing aside and promised to kick him out if there were no chocolates left when she showed up.

"Hey Shae," Kofi said just as she started disconnecting the call.

"Yeah?"

"I missed you."

The soft wistfulness in his voice made her laugh. "We were together last night."

"So? I miss you whenever you're not here," he replied. "See you when you get back."

Then he hung up as if his words didn't melt her already tender heart.

CHAPTER THIRTY-ONE

I miss you whenever you're not here.

Kofi grimaced as he opened Shae's fridge and pulled out the large glass jar she kept filled with miniature Hershey's nuggets. He grabbed a handful, careful to leave a few for Shae. He didn't want to risk seeing if she would make good on her threat to kick him out if he ate them all.

I miss you whenever you're not here.

Why the hell had he told her that? He *did* miss her when they weren't together. There was no way he could lie to himself about that. Not with the longing he felt as soon as he kissed her goodbye. He should've kept his mouth shut, though. Kofi didn't understand why he seemed to have vulnerability diarrhea where Shae was concerned. Maybe it was because she looked at him like she could see right into his heart and that made him feel comfortable instead of exposed. Whatever it was, Kofi found himself telling Shae things he would agonize over telling other people without a second thought.

I miss you whenever you're not here.

He smiled when he remembered the change in her voice when he spoke those words. His emotions were new, intense and sometimes overwhelming but at least Kofi knew he wasn't in it alone. That was terrifying enough to cause beads of sweat to form on his brow. Whatever decision he ended up making would hurt someone he loved. His mind stuttered over the word even as he acknowledged the absolute truth in them. The last five days were beyond anything he could have possibly hoped for. The moments he spent with Shae were magical. It didn't matter if they were going head to head in drunken games of Monopoly or Uno, plotting where they wanted to be in the next five years, exchanging funny childhood memories or if he was buried so deep inside her that he could feel her heart beating through her pussy. All that ever mattered was they were together in the intimate bubble they'd created. He and Shae went on a hike two evenings before and as they sat cuddled on the grass while the sunset cast purple and pink hues across the sky, Kofi suddenly realized that those moments were the most content he'd been in a very long time. He'd pulled her soft body closer to him and imagined how wonderful it would be to have her in his space. How much fun he'd have taking her to his favorite haunts in London and perhaps do a few weekend city breaks with her. He thought about waking up next to her in the morning and losing himself in her lush sweetness before he got ready for work. The best part of waking up would definitely not be Folgers in his cup. The almost dizzying happiness he felt when he thought about Shae coming back with him to London should have been enough to decide for him. He wished it were enough to decide for him. Trying to juggle Shae and Sheldon, while continuing to lie to Sheldon's face about what was really going on, was tiring as fuck. There were a few times when he wanted to just blurt it out and let the chips fall where they were supposed to but he couldn't make himself do it. He existed in this shadowy place where he assumed Sheldon would act the fool but he wasn't sure. He didn't have to decide unless Sheldon gave him an ultimatum. Kofi couldn't figure out where the line of loyalty ended and ridiculousness began. Was Sheldon saving him from a hellish childhood enough to sacrifice a very real shot at happiness with Shae?

He was still running the thoughts through his mind when he heard the front door close. He smiled when she finally padded into her bedroom. She wore leggings and an oversized shirt but damn if she wasn't still the sexiest thing he'd ever seen.

"I see you left some chocolate for me," she said as she started crawling on the bed. He tore his eyes away from her body and smiled. "I didn't want to risk being banished."

His body was on high alert when she straddled him and brushed her lips against his. "I would never banish you."

"That's the sweetest thing you've ever said to me," he teased. He grasped the back of her neck and pulled her towards him so he could taste her. The only thing more extraordinary and more luxurious than kissing Shae's soft, plump lips was feasting on those lips below her waist. His stomach tightened at the thought of just how much his tongue craved losing itself in her wet warmth, but he willed himself to slow things down. He would get there... eventually. He always did. But for now, he was going to enjoy the pleasure of kissing Shae's mouth. Her lips roved over his with enough eagerness that he could feel himself swelling in his pants. They had a rhythm going now. Kissing each other was no longer a heady exploration but it was just as sweet as it was familiar and Kofi fucking loved it. She teased his tongue with hers then trailed it along the inside of his lips before tugging it between her teeth. Kofi tightened his hold on her neck, pulling her even closer to him as he pressed his lips harder against hers. He kissed her until he struggled to breathe but he didn't draw his lips away. In those moments, kissing Shae was more important than drawing his next breath. She stared up at him with a small, sexy tilt of her lips.

"So damn beautiful," he murmured. He traced his finger along her cheek, jaw and down the front of her throat to her collarbone before he followed the same path his finger took with his lips and tongue. He chuckled as she bucked against him when his lips found that spot between her neck and collarbone that often drove her wild.

"I swear I didn't intend to jump you as soon as I came," she whispered as he ran his tongue over that spot again. Her voice was breathy and husky, and damn if that wasn't the biggest turn on.

"Trust me, love, I'm not complaining," he said. "At all."

He shifted them so she was lying on her back, hooking his thumbs in the elastic of her leggings and pulling them off. He kneeled between her legs, pushing a hand under her T-shirt and caressed her soft, warm skin before he licked his way down her pubic bone and the inside of her thighs. He licked her soft, wet folds and straight up her slit until he got to her clit. Kofi drew her clit into his mouth and sucked... lightly, then hard enough for her to jerk against him with a surprised yelp. Shae held the back of his head and pulled him into her pussy as he finally got to work. Eating Shae out was like dining at a fine establishment with too many options. Kofi never knew where he wanted to start. He feasted on her plump, wet flesh until Shae dug her heels into the bed and arched towards him. He sucked and licked her pussy's lips, laving it with the tender, devoted attention it deserved. He pleasured her until Shae's cries became whimpers and her body shook but he didn't let up. He didn't let up even when her sweet wetness coated his tongue and her cries became louder again.

"Kofi, please stop..."

He rose his head slowly, sliding his fingers between her legs and pinching her clit in quick bursts until she tried squeezing her legs shut.

"Do you really want me to stop?" he asked. She stared up at him for a few seconds, her beautiful mouth parted in pleasure, before she shook her head. He grinned. "Good girl."

Her pussy was wetter than he'd left it when he covered her with his mouth again, alternating between hard sucks and feather like nibbles, thrusting his tongue into her slit and licking lightly on the inside. He slid two fingers into her, thrusting in rotating motions while he laved attention on her clit. Her pussy was wet, slick, soft and swollen... so ready for his dick but Kofi wasn't done pleasing her yet. It didn't matter that he pressed so painfully against his pants that he had to stop fondling Shae's breasts so he could try to free his dick from its constraints. It didn't matter that he was already moist with precome. It didn't matter that if he left it any longer he might come as soon as he slid inside. All that mattered was the way Shae was squirming under him, clenching around his fingers, pulsing against his tongue. All that mattered was pleasing this woman who meant the world to him until she couldn't breathe, think or see straight. She came with a loud burst of curses, holding on to Kofi's head, trying to push him away from her. He grinned with the satisfaction of knowing he could make her lose control, not caring how goofy he probably looked with his beard soaked in her wetness.

"Watching you come is the best sight in the world," he confessed, running his hands over her stomach and then under the shirt to squeeze both of her breasts. She let out a long, raggedy sigh as she tried to sit up, failing on her first two attempts.

"I made you come so hard you can't even control your limbs," he teased as he helped her up. Shae rolled her eyes and sucked her teeth but there was no annoyance there.

"I was about to climb on that dick and take it for a ride," Shae said. She placed her palm to his chest and pushed him down on the bed.

He laughed. "And now?"

Her smile was bright as hell as she placed a knee on either side of him. Kofi expected her to slide down and cover his dick with her pussy but she didn't.

"But you talk too much," she said, smiling even harder. "Somebody should shut you up."

Her pussy was suddenly covering his face and her thighs, locked on either side of his head, muffled his response. She rocked her hips gently back and forth, pressing down hard like she was really trying to stop him from breathing. But Kofi didn't mind. He smacked her ass before his hands settled on her hips while he sucked her pussy as if the oxygen she was cutting off could be found there. Breathing was overrated anyway.

CHAPTER THIRTY-TWO

"We should get you some leather and a whip," Kofi teased, drawing Shae back into his arms. He kissed the side of her head. "You almost killed me, but that was sexy as hell."

She twisted in bed so she could face him. "I don't know what came over me."

Shae had no idea what possessed her to straddle Kofi's face but she didn't regret it. Maybe it was because he'd eaten her out with so much enthusiasm that it'd taken all of Shae's strength to stay upright. She didn't teach him the lesson she'd intended. She was the one who had to beg him to stop when he held her in place and laved her pussy with attention until Shae thought she would combust from it. Shae's entire world faded away when he lay her on her back and lifted one of her legs over his shoulder as he finally sank into her.

"Hold tight," he'd said. Shae laughed and blushed at the obvious call back to their first time. She heeded his warning, gripping the edge of the bed as he slammed into her so hard it took her breath away. She and Kofi had had slow, sensual sex; tender, romantic sex; hot, passionate sex... but this was something different. It was primal. It was instinctual. It was raw. Kofi fucked her. He fucked her until she couldn't process anything other than the way her breasts bounced violently and his balls slammed against her, creating a delicious friction that pushed her right to the edge. He squeezed her neck with the exact amount of pressure she liked while his other hand roamed over her breasts, twisting and pulling her nipples. Shae closed her eyes and welcomed an orgasm unlike anything she'd ever felt before. An orgasm unlike anything she thought she was capable of feeling. She couldn't scream. She couldn't squirm. She couldn't shriek. She couldn't do anything but allow the pleasure to pull her under. When she opened her eyes, Shae was fully prepared to see her spirit hovering over her body because Kofi should have done more than snatch her breath... he'd come after her soul. But what she saw was Kofi looking down at her with eyes filled with longing so intense that she couldn't look away from his gaze. He brought his forehead to hers and kissed her lightly before cupping her chin and fixing his eyes on her.

"You're mine," he said gruffly. "Do you understand?"

She swallowed hard and nodded, even as tears pricked the corner of her eyes. She wished it was so simple but they both knew it wasn't. She didn't bring up the obvious flaw with his declaration. She allowed herself the time to feel the absolute joy of the moment. Nearly half an hour passed before Shae couldn't ignore the elephant in the room any longer. She pushed herself up on her elbow. "I'm yours, huh?"

"It depends."

She smiled through the disappointment she felt. That was what she got for allowing herself to be swept up with the high emotions that came with good sex. Of course it was conditional. Kofi had made it clear that he would choose Sheldon if it came down to it.

"On what?" she said instead. She was filled with the sudden, nasty desire to make him say the words he probably didn't want to say. Her forehead furrowed when he smiled at her. "On whether I'm yours."

"Of course you are."

The truth spilled from her mouth with little thought but eventually she said, "You still have to talk to Sheldon…"

He didn't answer her right away. He pushed himself up off the bed and sauntered to the bedside table while Shae stared at him in confusion. He pulled her into his chest when he returned to the bed with his cellphone.

"I think it's time we book your ticket," he whispered.

"But…"

"I love Sheldon like a brother," he said. A wry smile crossed his handsome face. "I know it's an odd ass thing to say considering my feelings for you are not familial at all."

She laughed. Her heart felt like it had downed a can of Red Bull and was about to fly right out her chest.

"There's nothing wrong about what we're doing here," he said. "It will break our friendship either way. I'd probably resent the hell out of him if I have to give up seeing if this will be as amazing as my heart, soul, mind and dick think it will be."

Shae playfully punched him in the shoulder. "Your dick?"

He chuckled and pulled her closer to him. "Yeah. He's always got a lot to say." Then after a while he said, "What I'm saying Shae is I wouldn't forgive myself if I didn't see where this goes. Sheldon will have to deal with it."

"So where do we go from here?" Shae asked softly. Kofi cupped her cheeks and kissed her. "I guess it's time we talk to your brother."

CHAPTER THIRTY-THREE

"You're wearing a hole into the tiles," Kofi said. He reached out and grabbed Shae by the waist as she walked past him for what might have been the fifteenth time since he'd shown up to her house. She dressed in a pair of jeans and a white tank top but pulled her hair back into a tight bun. Anxiety rolled off her in waves. Kofi hated seeing her so worked up but he understood how she felt. His nerves were running high as hell too. She wrapped her hands around his waist and rested her head against his chest. He kissed the top her head and rubbed circles against the small of her back.

"It'll be okay," he soothed.

Shae looked up at him and Kofi wished he could kiss away the worry in her eyes.

"Are you sure you still want to do this? I understand if it is too much. I'll pay you back for the tick..."

He kissed away the words she was about to say. The last day and a half only reinforced everything he'd said to Shae. He wasn't going to give her up before they even got started. If that meant he was a selfish motherfucker, then he'd claim it. He'd print it on a shirt and on a mug. He'd take out a billboard. He was willing to be selfish for love. Kofi thought of the three calls from his mother that went unanswered while he had been driving over to Shae's house. Kofi could only handle one stress-inducing situation at a time so whatever his mother wanted to say had to take the back burner. The calls brought to the surface more of the guilt he felt after visiting her when he had to confront the true impact Sheldon's friendship had on his life. He'd waited for the uncertainty to cripple him like it had the last time but it didn't come. His resolve didn't waver. Kofi hoped like hell his friendship with Sheldon would survive the fallout, but he wasn't backing down. His best friend found a deep and genuine love with Kara and Kofi hoped he would be mature enough to not begrudge him and Shae that chance. He'd own that it was fucked up to sneak around with Shae instead of being upfront with Sheldon about it. But he'd never apologize for being with her. He'd never apologize for wanting a future with her. He'd never apologize for falling in love with her.

Falling in love.

The words had been on the tip of Kofi's tongue so often over the past few days that it almost physically hurt to swallow them down. He couldn't wait until he could hold her close and tell her the depths of what he felt for her.

"Everything will be okay," he said to her again. He'd tell her eventually but those three little words would have to wait until they were done fighting whatever storm Sheldon blew their way.

CHAPTER THIRTY-FOUR

Shae tried to find comfort in the warmth of Kofi's body pressed into hers but her mind wouldn't settle down. Her stomach cramped with unease. She wasn't ready. It didn't matter how many times Kofi promised her things would be okay. Could she really allow him to sacrifice the longest friendship of his life for a shot at a relationship with her? The girl who used to follow him around the house with heart eyes while he desperately tried to ward off her attention? She tried to massage away the tension forming at the base of her skull. Kofi kissed her forehead when he noticed her rubbing her neck before he brushed away her hands and did it himself. Her heart beat triple time. God. She was crazy about this man. The unease returned to her stomach with vicious force. What if this *thing* between them didn't stand the test of time? What if they drove each other crazy when she returned to London? Would he eventually resent her? She eased herself out of his embrace and started to ask the questions swirling around her head when a few raps at the door jolted her.

Shae glanced at her watch and frowned. "Why is he so early?"

Kofi tipped her chin up and kissed her. His lips lingered for a while before he pulled away. "Let's just get this over with."

She sighed. "Here goes nothing."

IT WAS SOMEHOW JUST as Shae expected, but also worse. Sheldon was standing on the porch looking at Kofi's rental parked outside when she opened the door. He turned to her with confusion written all over his face.

"Why is Kofi's rental parked outside? You invited him for something?"

She barely had a chance to start answering his question before he looked up and saw Kofi standing in the living room. Confusion gave way to something that looked like straight up anger.

"Let me go set the table," Shae said. She was anxious to divert his attention away from Kofi because nothing good could come out of the way the vein in her brother's neck jumped. Sheldon was having none of it. He shook his head and laughed bitterly.

"You fucking asshole."

He kept his full attention on Kofi even as Shae tried to grab his arm to lead him towards the kitchen.

"Sheldon..."

She and Kofi spoke at the same time. Sheldon looked at her for a few seconds and the disappointment she saw in his eyes made her stomach drop.

He turned his fury back to Kofi. "You fucking my little sister, man?"

Shae yanked his hand. "Hey. I'm right here. Please come sit down so we can talk."

Sheldon looked from Kofi to Shae as it slowly dawned on him what Shae's lunch invitation was all about.

"Yo," he said with a laugh. "This has to be a joke."

"Sheldon, just calm down so we can have the conversation we need to have."

This was from Kofi, who finally left his spot in the living room and started walking towards them.

"Have the conversation we need to have?" Sheldon's voice rose with each word. "You've lost your goddamn mind. There's no conversation to have. You've either been fucking Shae and lying to my face about it or you haven't. That's the only thing I need to know."

Sheldon was still standing in the foyer as if his feet had grown roots into the white tiles. Shae sighed. She guessed the revelation would not go the way she'd planned. Shae figured they'd at least get through lunch before they got around to the things they needed to discuss. Outkast was spot when they advised that as much as you could plan a pretty picnic there was no predicting the weather.

"We have been seeing each other," Kofi said. He stood next to Sheldon, and Shae half wanted to tell him to step away. She couldn't decide if Sheldon wanted to throttle him or punch him in the face, but everything about her brother spelled violence.

"*Seeing* each other?" Sheldon shook his head. "I trusted you. I can't even be mad at Shae. She's had a stupid crush on you for half her life. I just can't believe you'd take advantage of..."

Shae's anger flashed hot as any trepidation she'd been feeling drained away. She stood between Sheldon and Kofi, turning to look her brother dead in the face.

"What you're not about to do is infantilize me, Sheldon. I'm a grown ass woman capable of deciding whose dick I want in my pussy."

Shae didn't think a black man could go pale but Sheldon

seemed to right before her eyes. He'd started to respond when Kofi spoke up.

"You wouldn't know a thing if we were just fucking," he whispered. "We definitely wouldn't have to do all of this..."

He let his sentence hang in the air, willing Sheldon to put two and two together but her brother wasn't interested in doing the math.

"I'm going back to London with him," Shae said and instantly knew it was the worst thing to say.

"What the actual fuck is going on here?" Sheldon asked, but the question wasn't directed to Shae. He aimed each angry, snide syllable straight at Kofi.

"You're right. I lied to you," Kofi said. "I take that. I own that. You can be as angry as hell because I misled you. But I won't apologize for my feelings for Shae. Never that."

Sheldon shook his head. The loud brashness was gone from his voice when he spoke again. Guilt flowed through Shae at the hurt she heard there.

"I trusted you," he said. "Little things didn't add up but I refused to believe they could possibly mean what I suspected because you gave me your word."

"Sheldon..." Kofi started, but Sheldon sucked his teeth.

"What was this little domestic situation supposed to be about anyway?" he asked. He finally turned his attention to Shae. "Y'all seeking my blessing? Trying to convince me to be okay with the guy who grew up right beside us being with you like that?"

Shae straightened her spine and spoke in what she hoped was a clear voice despite the way her stomach knotted into itself. "No Sheldon. We're asking you to respect our decision to be together. We were hoping you could be supportive of two of the people you claim to love the most in this world finding happiness in each other."

Sheldon's face seemed to soften as he searched Shae's. Eventually, he chuckled and then laughed as he shook his head and started backing towards the door.

"I mean this from the bottom of my heart," he said in an icy tone. "Fuck y'all."

He slammed the front door so hard on his way out that the reverberation shook the decorative paintings lining the foyer's walls. Shae turned to Kofi, finally giving herself permission to release the tears welled in her eyes. "That did not go well."

He crossed the small distance between them and pulled her into his arms. She inhaled his scent, trying to find comfort in the familiarity of his body against hers. It didn't work. She'd expected Sheldon to be upset but not like that. Not explosively so. Her brother had never sworn at her. Not even in jest.

"Let's give him some time to cool off," Kofi suggested. She could hear the tension in his voice even though he was trying to be optimistic for her sake. She wanted to respond with one of the myriad worst-case scenarios in her mind but decided against it. They would cross those bridges when they got to them. Right now Shae wanted to eat lunch with Kofi and have him hold her until everything else faded away.

CHAPTER THIRTY-FIVE

Shae blinked against the bright sunlight filtering into the bedroom. Kofi was still asleep on his stomach with his cheek resting on his hands. She smiled. He looked uncomfortable as hell but he always somehow found that position during the night. She checked her phone and grimaced. It was nearly nine in the morning. Shae rarely slept so late but she wasn't surprised she and Kofi overslept. Yesterday was hard. Their disagreement with Sheldon still felt like stones in the pit of her stomach. She didn't want to be at odds with her brother but she had no idea how to fix things. She eased off the bed, slowing her motions to make sure she didn't wake Kofi. At least one of them deserved as much rest as their body would allow.

Shae moved into her house two years before and spent a lot of time ensuring each room was calming to her soul. The kitchen, with its high ceilings, was painted in the lightest shades of teal and fresh sunflowers sat on her countertops. Normally she'd sit at her breakfast nook overlooking the lush garden her mother helped her tend while sipping on her morning coffee and feel centered and at peace. She clenched her coffee mug and sighed. Peace was beyond her reach. Shae took the first sip of coffee, allowing the hot, bitter liquid to flow over her tongue. She thought back to everything Sheldon said and realized he hadn't said much at all. He spoke about feeling betrayed and hinted he believed Kofi took advantage of her but she still didn't have a clear idea of why her brother was so opposed to her and Kofi getting together. It was hard to reason with someone without knowing what exactly had them tripping out in the first place. She recalled Jada's horrified laughter when she gave her the details of what went down. Jada was, predictably, annoyed with Sheldon but she felt Shae and Kofi made the first mistake.

"Why the hell did you try to do this as a united front?" she'd asked, not even bothering to hide the incredulity in her voice. "You guys should have spoken to him separately."

She supposed Jada had a point. Sheldon came in blind and probably felt outnumbered. Yet, Shae didn't think there was a scenario under the sun that might have resulted in a different outcome. She checked her phone and grimaced when she realized all the messages she'd sent to Sheldon the night before remained unread. Why was he so damn stubborn? She started dialing Kara's number but stopped when she noticed Kofi coming into the kitchen. He wore only his boxers and poured himself a cup of coffee before he stretched his hands above his head and yawned. She dragged her eyes away from his toned abs and powerful legs. It said a lot that her body still reacted to him so... enthusiastically, even when her emotions were in crisis.

"I reached out for you and you were gone."

He slid into the chair closest to hers and placed a light kiss against her cheek. Her heart somersaulted in her chest. When Kofi said things like that, Shae's heart reacted enthusiastically to him too.

"I wanted to let you sleep," she said. "I've got a lot on my mind."

"That makes two of us."

Shae took a deep breath and prepared herself to ask Kofi the question that remained steady on her mind. She reached out so she could slide her hand into his and started to speak when he leaned over and kissed her.

"Yes," he whispered. "Nothing's changed. I'm still sure."

"How did you know I was going to ask that?"

He chuckled. "It's written all over your face."

He intertwined his fingers with hers and sighed. "Are *you* still sure?"

Shae nodded. She was sure she never wanted anything as much as she wanted this. She was sure they'd be good together. She just wished she could be sure Sheldon would come around. A small flicker of annoyance shot through her even as the thought floated into her head. She couldn't understand what Sheldon thought he had to lose if she and Kofi were together. Not to mention she hated the insinuation she was stupid enough to let a childhood crush cloud her judgment. What was going on between her and Kofi had nothing to do with their childhood. It was grown folks' stuff in the best ways possible.

"Sheldon is a grown ass man," Jada had said just before she'd disconnected the call. "Don't be pandering to his childish antics. What you and Kofi get up to is zero percent of his business."

Jada was right. Shae had half a mind to drive her ass over to Sheldon's house and tell him that to his face.

"Have you spoken to your parents?"

Kofi's unexpected question pulled her from her fantasy of yanking Sheldon's front door open and yelling at him.

"About Sheldon?"

He shook his head. "That you're planning on coming back with me on Saturday. That's not the thing you want to pop up and tell them on Friday night."

Shae muttered a curse under her breath. She'd been so

preoccupied and concerned about Sheldon's reaction that she hadn't thought about her parents. Her nerves were a hornet's nest in her chest. What if her parents reacted as badly as Sheldon did?

"Don't go panicking yet," Kofi warned. "Let's take things one step at a time."

Unrestrained panic filled her laughter. "The precedent isn't amazing."

His lips pulled into a reassuring smile as he squeezed her hand. "Do you want me to come with you?"

Shae recalled Jada's words and shook her head. "Nah. I think I should do this alone. Hopefully it goes better than with Sheldon."

Kofi raised his coffee mug to hers in a sardonic toast. "I can't see how it could go worse."

CHAPTER THIRTY-SIX

Kofi made Shae promise she'd call him as soon as she spoke to her parents when they parted ways early that afternoon. She'd suggested he just stayed in the house until she came back but Kofi was too restless for that. All of his calls to Sheldon were sent straight to voicemail and his messages left unread. He was willing to give Sheldon some time to cool down so they could talk through things rationally but his patience was wearing thin. Kofi's didn't bother checking the ID when his phone vibrated. He wondered if his mother's patience was wearing as thin for him as his patience was wearing for Sheldon. She'd called infrequently the night before but the calls increased as the hours wore on. Kofi signaled to the hotel's bartender who nodded at him before she returned with Kofi's third Mojito in the last hour. He'd barely taken a sip before his phone started ringing again. His finger hovered over the answer button, knowing answering the call would invite chaos. He remembered just how shitty he felt when he'd left his childhood home nearly a week before. He wasn't interested in a repeat, especially not when he was already stressing out about Sheldon and worrying about Shae. Yet, his curiosity increased with each unanswered call.

"Fuck it," he whispered.

He swiped to connect the call. "Yes, Deborah."

A few seconds passed before his mother answered. "I didn't expect you to pick up."

"Until a few seconds ago, neither did I," he admitted.

"I would like a few minutes of your time," she said in a slow, halting tone as if she reconsidered every word she said even as she spoke them. "Are you busy? Can you come over? I promise I won't be long but I have some things I want to say to you before you leave."

The thought of stepping back into that house made Kofi's throat tighten but he knew it'd be more torture wondering what his mother wanted to tell him so badly. Sheldon's house was on route to his childhood home so Kofi decided he would pop up on Sheldon when he finished listening to whatever Deborah wanted to get off her chest.

"I can be there in twenty minutes," he said. He hoped he didn't regret the hell out of either decision when all was said and done. Kofi waved down the bartender.

"Another Mojito?" the woman asked with a grin.

He nodded. "Make it strong."

DEBORAH WAS SITTING on the porch when Kofi pulled up. He killed the engine and took a deep breath. He'd decided he wouldn't argue with his mother. He didn't need her to validate his experience and he sure as hell didn't need her to help heal from it. Despite his pep talk, each step towards his mother felt like walking through quicksand. She didn't waste any time with pleasantries when he finally climbed the short set of steps leading to the large porch and sat in the wooden swing he used to spend half his evenings reading in as a child.

"I've been thinking about the conversation we had last week," she said by way of introduction. Her voice softened to barely a whisper. "I've been thinking about it a lot."

"I'm not going to apologize," he said. "If that's what…"

"I'm not asking you to," she started and then stopped to take a deep breath. She fixed him with a sad look as she spoke again. "I am sorry. You were right… you *are* right. Gerald wasn't fatherly to you. I hoped he would become more of the father I believed he could but that didn't happen. It was easier for me to pretend it couldn't possibly affect you that badly and that the financial situation he put us in was worth it. I don't know how much you remember about life before Gerald… but we struggled, Kofi. There was the part of me that was afraid I'd fail you if I tried to go it alone, but I suppose I failed you anyway."

She stared straight past him as if she couldn't bear to look at him when she continued. "And there was a part of me that loved my husband and didn't want to choose."

The anger that washed over Kofi was hot as the admission rubbed something raw within him. Then something else started poking its way through the dense fog that blanketed him: relief. He'd thought hearing her admit Gerald's poor treatment of him and her complicity in it wouldn't affect him at all. He didn't expect it to feel so… freeing. The knot in his chest loosened slowly.

"Thank you," he said, pushing himself off the swing. "I am happy we had this talk."

He started towards the gate when Deborah called after him.

"Kofi?"

"Yes."

"I hope you can find it in your heart to not hate me."

Her words were a sucker punch to the gut.

"I don't hate you," he said. "I've felt abandoned by you. In a lot of ways, I still do."

"Is there anything I can do to fix that?" she asked.

Kofi considered the question. A few days ago he wouldn't have had to think, the answer would have been a clear no. But right now he wasn't sure. He thought of the therapy sessions he'd already booked online. Perhaps in a few months he'd have a better answer.

"I honestly don't know," he admitted. "But you will be the first to know."

He hoped his small smile would be enough to take the edge off, for her to know he wasn't trying to hurt her. He just truly had no clue.

Her face crumpled but she fixed it so quickly Kofi almost thought he'd imagined it. He started leaving when she called out to him and he turned to look at her expectantly for a few seconds before she blurted out.

"Do you think you could let me know when you get back safely?"

He nodded even though he doubted that was what she truly wanted to say. She confirmed his suspicions a few seconds later when she asked in a soft, shaking voice. "Can I hug you goodbye?"

Kofi stiffened. The request surprised him, but not more than the pang of longing that hit him when he thought of hugging his mother. He hesitated slightly before he took two long strides towards her and enveloped her in his arms. She still smelled like Elizabeth Taylor's 'White Dimonds' just like she did in his childhood. She wrapped her hands around his waist and squeezed. They stood there in that embrace for what felt like forever before Deborah stepped out of Kofi's arms and reminded him of his promise to let her know when he got back to London safely.

It wasn't until Kofi sat in his rental, trying to let all the emotions pass through him, that he realized he hadn't hugged his mother in over a decade.

CHAPTER THIRTY-SEVEN

Shae followed the captivating scents of stewed oxtail into the kitchen when she arrived to her parents' house. She stood for a few minutes watching her mother move easily around the kitchen while she hummed to herself, checking the pots that were bubbling on the stove and stopping every so often to taste the meal she was preparing.

"How long are you going to stand there?" her mother suddenly called out. Grace didn't even turn around as she opened the oven and checked on whatever she had baking.

Shae chuckled. "How did you know I'm here?"

Her mother turned around this time, deftly removed her apron and smiled widely at her daughter. "I've got eyes in the back of my head. Isn't that what you and Sheldon swore by while you were growing up?"

"Thankfully I've aged up in commonsense as well as years."

Grace laughed. Shae loved her mother's laugh. For a woman who was dainty and usually so prim and proper, her laughter was a boisterous wave.

"What do I owe this sneak visit?" her mother asked. "And you came just as I got finished cooking too."

"You going to fix me a plate?" she said in a sweet voice while her mother busied herself turning off the stove.

"I'll fix you a plate to go," her mother replied. "It's too early for lunch."

Shae's tone was playful when she responded. "It is never too early for good food."

Her mother brushed off the compliment, moving towards the toaster oven. She pulled out two muffins that had been warming and offered one to Shae before pushing a jar of strawberry jam across the island.

"This can hold you over until lunchtime."

"Is Daddy around?" Shae asked. Asking after the food was a losing battle. Her mother wouldn't let her anywhere close to the oxtail until she thought it was an appropriate time.

"He's reading in the backyard."

"Can we take the muffins outside? I want to talk to both of you real quick."

Her mother stared at her with open curiosity but Shae only planned to go through everything once, so she grabbed the strawberry jam and headed for the kitchen door with her mother trailing right behind her.

Her father was resting in the large, bright orange hammock hanging between two mango trees in the backyard. He was so enthralled in the novel he read that he barely looked up when Shae stood over him.

"Hey Daddy."

He raised a finger and continued reading for a few seconds before he looked up from the book.

"Hey Care Bear," he smiled. "Just had to finish that paragraph."

She leaned down to give him a tight hug, almost toppling them both over in the hammock.

"I didn't know you were planning to stop by," Garvin said.

"Apparently she needs to talk to us," her mother said. "Let's move to a bench so we can all sit."

They'd been sitting on one of the picnic benches for nearly five minutes with Garvin giving a recap of the thriller he was reading before he finally turned to Shae and asked what she had on her mind. She quickly swallowed the muffin she'd been picking on.

"I'm going to London for a few months this weekend."

"I didn't know you had any travel planned," her mother commented. Grace liked to keep on top of Shae's travel diary and she was happy to oblige her mother since she was usually the one taking care of her plants when she was away.

"It was a kind of last minute thing," Shae said. "Unexpected."

"Is it a brand trip?" her father asked. Shae smiled at how satisfied he looked with himself for being able to speak the lingo.

"You've been watching YouTube videos, Daddy?" she asked. "I didn't think you knew what a brand trip was."

Her father laughed. "I don't have to watch YouTube videos. I listen to you and your mother talk enough."

"I'm going to have to be more careful about what I gossip to mommy about now I know you pay attention," she teased. "But, no. It's not a brand trip. It's personal, actually. I'm going back with Kofi."

She spoke the last sentence in one quick breath and found her parents staring at her with a myriad of expressions plastered on their faces when she finally looked up at them.

"With Kofi?" Garvin asked. If he raised his eyebrows any higher they would slide right off his forehead. She glanced at her mother but couldn't read her expression so she turned her attention back to father. "We've been kinda seeing each other. My job is flexible so we figured we could give ourselves some more time to hang out if I went back with him."

"Hang out?" her father asked. "I'd hope Kofi's clearer about his intentions with you."

"Garvin," her mother interrupted. "Keep out the young people's business. If they are planning to *hang out,* let them *hang out.*"

A small smile flickered across her face. "Was Kofi why you were so tired at your birthday brunch?"

"What? No," Shae squealed. "Mom!"

"We're all adults here," Grace said as if she was aggrieved by Shae not wanting to discuss her sex life. She stole a glance at her father and her heart sank when she realized he was still looking annoyed as hell.

"Are you mad, Daddy?" she asked softly.

He started talking but stopped like he was trying to decide if Shae would receive what he would say well.

"You can say whatever you want to say," she said. She dug her fingernails into her palms as she waited to hear what he'd been holding back.

"You're an adult capable of making your own decisions and you often make great ones. I just don't like the idea of you traveling halfway across the world to be with someone who isn't sure what he wants from you."

"*That* is what bothers you? That he isn't my boyfriend?"

Her father nodded. "Yes. What else is there to complain about? I've known Kofi since he was a boy and I have no doubts he'd treat you well and keep you safe while you are with him, but..."

The laughter that exploded from her was so sudden and so loud that both Garvin and Grace looked startled. She clapped her hand over her mouth as the laughter subsided.

"Sorry," she said. "I didn't mean to laugh. You don't have to worry. Kofi and I are pretty sure about where we want this to go.

If he was still living here we'd continue going on dates, but he needs to get back to work."

"And you can work from anywhere..." her mother added. This time Shae didn't have any problems reading the expression on her mother's face. Glee. Absolute glee. Her shoulders sagged with relief. Her parents' reactions were far better than she dared hope for.

"So you both approve?" she asked. "I was so worried you'd be mad."

"You're not sixteen," Garvin said. "You don't need our approval to choose who you want to date."

Her mother nodded as Garvin spoke before she asked. "Why would think we would be mad?"

"Sheldon lost his shit," she confessed. "He's not talking to either of us. I started wondering if I was doing the right thing."

Her father sucked his teeth. "Does being with Kofi make you happy?"

She couldn't stop the wide smile that spread across her face. "So much."

"Then leave Sheldon to himself until he comes around. I can't think of any legitimate reason he could have for being upset..."

"What if he doesn't come around?" she asked. That was what it all came down to, didn't it? It still made her a bit sick with worry when she thought she might lose her brother forever.

Her mother slathered jam on her muffin and looked up at Shae with a smile. "That sounds like a Sheldon problem not a you problem. Unless you're actively harming someone, their reaction to how you live your life is their problem. I'll happily go over there and put the fear of God in him if you want me to."

Her father laughed. "You know she will."

Shae didn't doubt that Grace would do just that but she

didn't want to drag her parents any further into this than they already were.

"I'll keep my options open," she said with a small smile. "But I think it's time for me and Sheldon to have a long, hard talk."

CHAPTER THIRTY-EIGHT

Shae spent the entire drive to the house Sheldon and Kara shared reciting what she wanted to say to him. She'd thought she'd come up with the perfect speech but everything she'd rehearsed flew from her head when she was finally face to face with her brother. Kara was the one who'd answered the door and offered Shae a sympathetic smile before telling her Sheldon was in the living room.

The TV was blaring but Sheldon wasn't even looking at it. He stared off into space and didn't even notice she'd come into the living room until she flopped down next to him on the couch.

"Good afternoon, brother," she said, deciding it might be better to start off with some light teasing. "Unless you've resigned from the position."

She expected her comment to draw at least a small smile from Sheldon but he continued staring ahead stone-faced.

Shae felt the patience she'd been determined to keep slip a notch.

"I've given you some time to cool off and now it's time to discuss this like rational human beings."

"I don't have anything left to say."

Shae rolled her eyes. "Whatever, Sheldon. You didn't say anything in the first place. I still have no damn idea what your problem is with me dating Kofi."

He turned to her with his eyes flashing full of tired patience. "No damn idea?"

"I never thought you'd become one of those Neanderthal-minded, annoying ass brothers who feel like it's their business to mind their sister's pussy."

Sheldon grimaced. "Please keep your pussy out of this."

Shae didn't give a damn how uncomfortable the conversation was making Sheldon.

"Isn't my pussy the issue here? Cause I swear you're throwing a tantrum because I let your best friend to stick his dick in it."

"You're being silly as hell, Shae."

"Me?" Shae asked pointed to herself. "I, Shae Marie Abbott, am being silly? And you're the poster child for rationality, right? Get the fuck outta here."

"Look, I told Kofi I didn't want him coming on to you like that and he lied his ass off about it."

"That isn't your call to make," she said. She couldn't stop the anger from spilling into her voice.

"He is my best friend," Sheldon shot back as if that explained everything.

Silence stretched out between them until Shae finally asked, "Are you in love with Kofi, Sheldon?"

He stared at her for a few seconds before his lips quirked and he began to laugh. And laugh. And laugh.

"I tell you to stop being silly and *that* is what you come up with?"

Shae could feel the tension in the room slide down a notch. She breathed a small sigh of relief. "It's the only fucking thing that makes sense right now to be honest. Are you secretly pining over Kofi so you're jealous and low key hate me?"

Sheldon was still laughing. "I high key hate you for being a straight fool. My fiancée, who owns my soul, is somewhere in this house right now. But most importantly, Kofi is annoying as fuck. Who would want to date him?"

Shae made a face and stuck her tongue out at him. "I can think of one person off the top of my head. She's just confused as hell because the brother, she loves for some reason, is being a dick about it. What's really going on? Do you think he'll dog me out?"

"Nah, never."

The answer rolled off Sheldon's tongue without him having to think about it. He must have seen the confusion written all over Shae's face because he shook his head and sighed like he regretted answering her.

"Jesus Christ, Sheldon. I'm so damn lost. What is the problem?"

"Kofi is great. You are great. Maybe you are great together. I don't know. I don't want to think about that. The problem is that relationships don't always work out. Sometimes amazing people are horrible together. Sometimes people who are great together grow toxic. What happens then? Kofi is the sibling I wish I had," Sheldon flashed her a lopsided grin. "No offence, but you know my three-year-old self wanted to pitch you out the window when you weren't the brother I ordered."

"I hate you," Shae giggled. When Sheldon reached over and playfully flicked her nose, a habit that drove her crazy growing up, she finally felt like things would be okay.

"Honestly Shae," Sheldon sighed. "What do I do if things implode between y'all? I'd have to choose between my sister and the brother the Universe owed me."

Shae's heart plummeted as everything finally made sense in ways it should've from the start.

"You can't get rid of me." She edged closer to him and rested her head on his shoulder. "You can't get rid of Kofi either. We'd never expect you to choose between us even if things don't work out. He *is* your brother, but he sure as hell isn't mine."

Sheldon jerked back. "Please do not put that imagery in my head."

Shae hugged him tight. "Are you still mad with me, Don-Don?"

"I'm not mad with you," he said after a while. "Kofi betrayed my trust, though."

She rolled her eyes. "He might have withheld some things from you, but it's only because he was afraid you'd act like an asshole... and, well, you did."

"I asked him straight up if something was going on between you two and he lied."

"So you are even then."

Sheldon cocked his head to the side and raised an eyebrow. "Even?"

"The only reason Kofi ever started thinking we could be a thing was because you were such a shitty ass friend to him when he came home for Christmas the year you started dating Kara."

"I was what?"

She chuckled. "Wow. You didn't realize? I guess he never lit up your ass for it. You ditched him, cancelled on him... sometimes *forgot* to cancel on him for the entire three weeks he was here. You know who he was spending his time with? Me. And during that time he realized I'd somehow evolved from just being your annoying little sister."

He made a rude noise in his throat. "I don't know Shae. You're still a pain in the ass."

"We spent all Christmas feeling each other but he never made a move out of respect for you."

"He should've kept that same energy," Sheldon mumbled and Shae punched him in the shoulder.

"I'll beat your ass," she threatened. "And mommy and daddy won't care cause they think you're dead wrong too."

Sheldon's eyes widened. "You went tattling to the parents? Wow. I don't even know you."

"Are you seriously going to keep up with the attitude?" she asked, suddenly tired of the back and forth. "You'd prefer to be bitter? You're willing to lose Kofi's friendship on the odd chance that you might in the future? Tell me now so I don't waste anymore time... I've got packing to do."

The last jab was childish as hell, but Shae couldn't bring herself to care. She understood the fear about being caught between them if things didn't work out. She would feel that way if the situation were reversed and it was Sheldon and Jada trying to work their way into a relationship. But she wouldn't antagonize them. Not when there was a possibility things might work out.

"You know what?" she said with a sigh. "I'm going to go."

Sheldon grabbed her arm when she started getting up.

"I won't be mad forever," he said. "I *can't* be mad forever. You guys are some of the most important people in my life. I just need some time to process it."

Shae nodded, feeling the irritation flow out of her. That was fair. She would be unreasonable if she expected anything more.

"I understand," she said. She allowed Sheldon to pull her into a hug. "Process all you need."

"So London, huh? Have you mapped out fifty thousand blog posts to capitalize on your time there?"

Shae laughed. "They can't say you don't know your sister."

"I love you, Shae," he said. "Never doubt that."

She kissed his cheek. "I love you too. I might not be what you ordered but I'm the fucking best."

Sheldon was shaking his head and laughing when she finally got up from the couch and headed from the living room. Her shoulders felt so much lighter than they had when she'd first come. Things wouldn't sort themselves out immediately but she now knew they would be okay.

"Y'all talked it out?"

Kara was tossing a Frisbee to their German Shepherd, Ziva, in the yard when Shae emerged from the house.

"We're getting there."

"Don't worry," she said, taking the Frisbee the dog fetched from her mouth and scratching behind her ears before throwing it again. "He won't be in his feelings forever. He's already running out a steam. He mentioned Kofi nearly six times today alone."

Shae laughed. "We'll just give him some more time…"

She'd barely finished her sentence when she saw Kofi's rental pulling into the drive. Kara smiled mischievously. "I see y'all already thinking like each other."

Her body went warm all over when Kofi emerged from the car wearing a fitted green T-shirt and Bermuda shorts like she hadn't woken up in his arms that morning.

"Hey Shae Butter," he whispered, leaning in to plant a kiss on her cheek. "I didn't expect to see you here."

"I didn't expect to be here, but I decided I was going to force Sheldon to listen to me."

He smiled and her stomach tightened a little. "I'm here to do the same thing."

She tiptoed and brushed her lips against his. "I'll see you later, then?"

"Definitely. I met up with my mother today and I have a lot of shit to tell you."

She had a dopey ass smile on her face as she watched Kofi pull Kara into a hug before heading into the house.

"Kofi is old, old news. I only liked him when I was a kid," Kara teased, mimicking Shae's voice. Her cheeks flushed when she remembered her defensive reaction to Kara pointing out the chemistry between her and Kofi at the engagement party.

She grinned. "He's definitely breaking news now."

CHAPTER THIRTY-NINE

"Is this gang up on Sheldon day?"

Kofi barely made it into the house before he almost bumped into Sheldon heading towards the living room with a can of beer.

"Offer me a beer, Sheldon," Kofi said and smiled when his best friend glared at him. "We need to talk."

Sheldon hesitated before he turned around and headed to the fridge. He took out another can of beer but left it on the counter instead of handing it to Kofi. Kofi rolled his eyes. "Few things look good on you but petty is one of your worst looks."

He took his sweet time sauntering to the kitchen, opening the can of Carib beer and taking a long sip before he turned to Sheldon. "I'm sorry."

"That doesn't unfuck my sister," Sheldon muttered.

"Oh... I'm not sorry about *that*. I will never be sorry about that."

Sheldon placed his can of beer on the counter. "Suddenly not very thirsty anymore."

"I said this already but you need to get it through your head.

This isn't about the sex. I wouldn't have needed to say anything to you if I thought this was just going to be a fling."

Sheldon started to respond but Kofi cut him off.

"I need you to listen to me," he breathed. "Truly listen to me. You were right about back in Jamaica when she came to visit. It was the first time I looked at Shae and something inside me shook free. I pushed it to the side because I didn't know how to deal with it. Then you started pointedly warning me off Shae and I pushed it even further away because I didn't want to jeopardize our friendship. But I couldn't help but notice that she was funny, smart and well... sexy as hell."

He chuckled when Sheldon scowled. "Fix your face. It's a fact. I was able to dead that spark of interest until..."

"... a couple years ago you came home and I was caught up in Kara so you ended up spending a bunch of time with Shae and suddenly you're in love."

"Yes," Kofi whispered. "All of that is true."

Sheldon's eyes widened a little. "*All* of it."

Kofi nodded. "Every single word."

Sheldon leaned against the counter and shook his head. "Why weren't you just honest with me?"

"I'm sorry for *that*," Kofi admitted. "I guess I was just scared. I didn't want us to fall out, but I knew Shae and I could have something special. I didn't want to miss out on that. I already regretted the opportunity I let pass us by."

"You tricked me into helping you plan a date with my sister," Sheldon said as if it suddenly dawned on him. He was laughing after a few seconds. "You ain't shit."

Kofi smiled. "But do you remember all the things I told you about this woman I refused to name? You clowned me the entire time about being totally gone, head over heels and suggested I made up my mind that my single days were ending. You even suggested a double wedding. Remember?"

"I can't say it rings a bell," Sheldon said. After a while he continued, "I reacted badly..."

Kofi chuckled. "You think?"

"Shae was obsessed with you as a kid but it didn't bother me because you never paid her any mind. I saw the way you looked at her in Jamaica and that was when I started worrying something like this could happen."

"So you started warning me off?"

"I didn't want you guys to hook up, things end badly and then I'd have to kill you or cut you off."

Kofi laughed. "You didn't have to think too hard about that, did you?"

"She's my sister, man. You didn't stand a chance."

Kofi placed his hand over his chest and winced exaggeratedly. "I'm wounded, bruv."

He rest his can of beer on the counter before he met Sheldon's gaze and held it. "You don't have to worry about things ending badly, Sheldon. They won't."

"Is that so?" Sheldon asked.

"You're looking at this all wrong," Kofi said with a small nod. "You keep saying that I'm the brother you never had. Well... sit down, be patient and watch Shae make me your brother for real because the only intention I have towards your sister is making her mine forever."

Sheldon stood there with his mouth parted for what felt like an eternity before he lifted the can of beer to his lips. He took a long gulp before he said, "Well, damn."

CHAPTER FORTY

"Today has been a long ass year," Kofi said. He shook his head as if he was still trying to make sense of the crazy day. Shae didn't blame him. She could hardly make sense of the day herself. They snuggled on the couch flicking through the YouTube app on Shae's smart TV trying to find something interesting to watch but Shae's mind was still racing. She'd worried instantly when he told her he'd met up with his mother again. She didn't expect Kofi and Deborah to have had a conversation that might be the start of the closure he needed more than he thought. She'd watched the tension slowly seep out of him as he recounted the events.

"I'm so happy she stopped gaslighting you," she'd said. "I hope you still plan to go through with the therapy."

He dropped a kiss on her forehead. "Somebody made sure I paid for my sessions up front and I don't like to waste money."

They'd spoken a bit more about what Kofi hoped to get out of therapy before they moved on to talking about Sheldon. It would take time before things returned to whatever new normal would come from their relationship. But things would get there. And that was all that mattered.

"Today had so much potential for disaster that I feel we should be out celebrating how things turned out. It's not even five yet and we're about to fall asleep right here on this couch," she teased.

"How about tacos and a movie?" he suggested.

"What's even on at the movie right now?" Shae asked while reaching for her phone to pull up the cinema's website. Kofi grabbed the phone from her and laughed. "Not everything needs planning. We'll just watch whatever's about to start when we're done eating."

"Are you sure you want to do that?"

Shae couldn't hide the skepticism in her voice or the small frown on her face. Kofi leaned forward and kissed the frown away. "It'll be an adventure, Shae Butter."

She smiled. "Okay. You win. Let's do it."

"MAYBE WE SHOULD'VE CHECKED."

Shae glanced at Kofi's distressed face and laughed even harder. The tacos they had at the small, brightly colored restaurant next to the cinema were great but by the time they made the short walk to the box office the only movie about to start was some animated kids film that looked like it would bore anybody over five years old to death.

"You promised me a movie," she teased. "And I intend to collect."

"I didn't expect this to be the only option," he muttered. "You really want to see this knockoff version of *Finding Nemo*?"

She shrugged and pointed him to the small line of parents and overly energetic children.

"Is anybody over there over seven?" Kofi asked.

"We'll be," Shae said as laughter overtook her again. It took less than ten minutes before they were seated in the back of the cinema. There were about fifteen kids and their caretakers scattered across the very front. Shae chuckled, remembering when she was young enough to think the best views in a cinema came from sitting as close to the screen as her mother would allow.

"I can't believe we're really watching this," Kofi said. He reached into the large popcorn they shared as the first trailers started. Shae raised the armrest between them so she could cuddle closer to him.

"It'll be an adventure," she mocked and then chuckled when he threw a kernel of popcorn at her.

"You're having fun with this, aren't you?" he asked. Shae smirked.

"Am I having fun watching you regret doing the exact opposite of something I suggested?" she asked sweetly. "Never."

"We'll see who gets the last laugh," Kofi shot back. Shae rest her head against his chest and didn't pay any attention to his threat. She didn't pay any attention until she felt Kofi's fingertips trailing down her side and slipping under her blouse a quarter way through the movie that was shaping up to be the *Finding Nemo* ripoff Kofi accused it of being.

She squirmed against him. "What are you doing?"

"Pay attention to the movie," he said while fingers continued trailing up her bare skin and skimmed the underside of her breast. Her body reacted instantly. She squirmed against him again.

"Kofi..."

He ignored the warning in her voice and responded in a light, amused tone. "Yes, Shae Butter? Just focus on the movie. Everybody else is."

He wasn't lying. They were the only people sitting in the final three rows of the cinema and all the children seemed engrossed with the movie and their caretakers were preoccupied with their phones. The movie truly was boring as fuck. Maybe that was why she didn't protest when his fingers moved from the underside of her breasts and pinched her nipples through her bra. Her breaths quickened as he rolled the hardened nub between his fingers. She moaned into his chest and felt his body vibrate with laughter. That didn't stop her from twisting in the chair so he had better access to her breasts. Her eyes fluttered closed as he caressed her.

"Sit up for me," he said. Her body responded to his command before she could even think about it. She was barely sitting up when his lips were on hers moving roughly as his hand inched its way under her dress and straight inside her panties. Kofi's lips muffled Shae's groan. He pulled back and she could make out the outline of a smile spreading across his face when two fingers slid inside. Her breath caught in her throat as he continued thrusting in and out of her, teeth grazing the flesh of her neck in such an unhurried, unconcerned way that Shae wondered if he forgot they were in the middle of a half-filled cinema while an animated story of a porcupine finding her way home played on the screen.

"This is a much better show," he murmured against her ear before gently sinking his teeth into her earlobe. Oh, he didn't forget. He just didn't give a damn. He rubbed her clit with his thumb and Shae lost the ability to think. He held the back of her neck and pulled her into him, capturing her mouth and kissing away her frantic, increasingly loud moans as she arched into him while her pussy clenched around his fingers.

"Come for me," he whispered. His fingers increased the pressure and speed until her body couldn't resist the inevitable any longer. His lips thankfully muffled the curses that streamed from her mouth as she came. He squeezed her clit lightly before he withdrew his fingers and settled back into his seat. Kofi dug his fingers into the tub of popcorn and popped a few into his mouth.

"Oh my gosh, Kofi," Shae laughed. "You could have used your other hand."

He reached out for her and pulled her against his chest. "Why? You make it taste better."

CHAPTER FORTY-ONE

"I don't even know who you are anymore."

"Shut up, Jada," Shae laughed. Her best friend was helping organize her things as she got ready for London. She'd said she wouldn't leave packing until the last minute but despite her good intentions she was now frantically trying to make sure she didn't forget anything important. Just thinking about spending three months with Kofi made her stomach clench with excitement and nerves. She looked forward to waking up to Kofi every day and exploring London through his eyes. They'd spent most of the night before cuddling in bed while making plans of how they wanted to spend the next three months. She'd contemplated cancelling her Jamaica Carnival trip but Kofi suggested they made a vacation out of it. They'd narrowed down eight European cities for weekend breaks. She was truly excited about those city trips because they would provide not only excellent vlogging and blogging content but also the bonding experience of exploring unknown places together. She couldn't wait to stumble down streets in countries neither she nor Kofi could speak the language of half drunk on wine.

"You just be out here fucking all willy-nilly in public," Jada continued, but Shae could hear the absolute glee in her voice. "Y'all could've scarred one of those children for life."

Shae continued going through the pile of clothes they'd pulled out of her closet and tried to focus on cutting the pile down to a suitable amount. The conversation shifted from Kofi to general gossip until it finally landed on Sheldon.

"Did I ever tell you he made a pass at me?" Jada said with a smirk and Shae playfully threw a jumpsuit she'd been assessing at her head.

"I swear if you say that one more time."

"But he's got his head out his ass now, right?"

Shae thought for a while before she told Jada he had. The day before he'd surprised the hell out of her, Kofi and even Kara when he called and asked if they wanted to go to lunch together.

"As in with me and Kofi?" she'd asked cautiously.

"Yeah. I guess your lil' boyfriend can come too."

They'd met up for drinks and pizza and although the conversation was stilted occasionally and some moments were downright uncomfortable, Shae could see that her brother was trying and that was truly all she and Kofi could ask for. Sheldon hugged her tightly after they returned to their cars and whispered, "Don't hesitate to call me if he's ever on any shit. I'll always go to battle for you."

Her heart expanded as she tried her best to keep tears from falling.

"I love you, Sheldon." She hugged him as tightly as she could.

"Right back at you, brat," he shot back before turning to Kofi. "You better take care of my little sister."

"With my life."

And Shae knew he meant every word of that. Jada was grinning broadly when she finished recounting the lunch date.

"I take back everything I said about birthday sex not counting," she laughed. "You birthday sexed your way into your happily ever after."

Jada caught the pair of shorts Shae sent flying in her direction. "I'll miss you but I'm so damn excited for you."

"I'm kinda scared," Shae admitted out loud for the first time. "What if everything goes to shit?"

Jada shook her head. "Then you hop your pretty ass on the next flight home and send Sheldon back to collect Kofi's soul, but we both know it won't come to that. I've seen the way you look at each other. The only thing that's going to come out of this is you will end up splitting time between here and London before you abandon us for good."

Shae couldn't get Jada's words out of her head as they continued packing for the next three hours. When Kofi showed up later that night and pulled her into a hug before pressing a kiss to the side of her head and telling her how much he missed her, Shae decided she wouldn't worry about the future. She would experience each beautiful moment fully and let the chips fall where they were meant to fall. Kofi reached out for her while he slept and Shae's heart screamed that this was exactly where the chips were meant to fall. Them intertwined together, hearts beating in time and the air around them vibrating with the love they were yet to announce but showed in every way.

CHAPTER FORTY-TWO

Kofi hoisted the last of Shae's bags on the scale and waited for the weight to pop up. They both had a running bet that every single one of her bags would be overweight. Kofi was two for three. The extra bag came in under British Airways' prescribed weight limit, just barely. Shae flashed him a large, triumphant smile and his heart stuttered in his chest. He didn't think he'd ever get used to the surge of adoration that pulsed through his body when Shae did some of the most random things. It was getting harder and harder not to spill the truth of the feelings that were so bright and so big that his heart could barely handle them. He spent the rest of the check-in process trying to imagine how she might react to him telling her he loved her. Would she believe him? Would she think it was too soon? Would she freak out? Or would she say those sweet words back? There were times he'd catch her looking at him with so much raw emotion in her eyes that he found it hard to believe she wasn't feeling the same things that consumed him.

"Is everything okay?"

Her pretty lips pulled into a frown as her hands went to his back as if to steady him from whatever unseen problems she thought he faced.

"I've never been better," he said. Those lips curved into a relieved smile and the words tumbled out his mouth before he could stop them.

"God, you're perfect," he murmured. "I love you."

Her eyes widened slightly before her smile grew. All the people bustling around them trying to check into their different airlines disappeared when she tiptoed, kissed Kofi deeply and whispered. "I love you too."

Relief flowed through him. "Thank God. It would have been an awkward as hell eight hours if I'd freaked you out. I was waiting for a better time…"

She cut him off with another kiss and he stopped speaking so he could savor her. He wrapped his hands around her waist and squeezed her into him, relishing the way her body felt against his and how her tongue felt in his mouth.

"Please get a damn room."

Sheldon's voice seemed suspiciously close as he pulled away from Shae. Sheldon stood less than two feet away with Kara close by and his and Shae's parents behind them. A lump of emotion rose to his throat but he played it off with a sharp cough. He definitely hadn't expected Sheldon to come to see them off.

"Close your eyes if you don't want to look at it," he teased, hoping the joke landed well.

Sheldon smirked. "That's a better alternative to having to burn my eyes out with caustic acid."

"Spare us the drama," Shae piped in, stepping out of Kofi's arms and into her brother's. "I don't know where mommy and daddy got you from."

They bantered back and forth for a while before the six of them headed to a small restaurant in the main terminal of the

VC Bird International Airport and had a drink. The mood was light and by the time Shae and Kofi headed to the escalators leading to immigration, Sheldon was threatening to send Grace to London to cramp their sex lives. They said their goodbyes in a flurry of hugs and well wishes and Sheldon allowed Shae to step on the escalator before he pulled Kofi aside. "Be good to her."

"You don't have anything to worry about."

Sheldon nodded. "I love you like a brother but I can turn into Cain real quick."

Kofi laughed. "I got it."

He gave Sheldon a small salute and hugged Kara, Garvin and Grace before he joined Shae on the escalator.

"Sheldon is threatening you again?" she asked with a laugh when he wrapped his hands around her.

"Threats of biblical proportions," he said with a chuckle. He interlaced his fingers through hers as they waited for their turn to go through immigration. He smiled at her when the arrow lit up, showing they needed to head to the fourth immigration booth.

"Ready for our adventure?"

She smiled that smile he loved so much. "Since I was twelve."

SHAE TRIED hard to keep her excitement under control but she failed once the flight started boarding.

"I can't believe this is really happening," she said, looking up at Kofi to see if he was as dumbstruck as she was.

He grinned at her. "Neither can I, but I'm grateful as hell it is."

Shae smiled. He was truly the sweetest and always knew

the right thing to say. He squeezed her hand as they found their seats and pulled her into him as soon as they sat down.

The first half of the flight passed with their favorite game of outlining all the things they planned to do. Their plans had changed ever so slightly from the last time they'd had the conversation and she chuckled thinking about how much they would likely change during the three months. Kofi grinned at her halfway through the flight when most passengers seemed to be asleep and the lights in the cabin dimmed. She could tell from the way his smile spread so wide that his dimples were deeper than usual and the way he'd started tracing circles on her leg that he was about to say something risque.

"Have you ever thought of joining the Mile High Club?" he asked. Jada's teasing remarks about how wanton she was with Kofi came flooding through her mind. The teasing remarks weren't enough to stop her pussy from purring to life.

"Suppose we get caught?" she asked, even though the idea intrigued the fuck out of her.

"Supposed we don't?"

And that was all it took for Shae to be sneaking to an empty lavatory with Kofi, giggling hard when she thought about how horrified Jada would be when she told her about it. He pressed her against the door of the too small space and kissed her until she was trying to arch her body into him.

"We definitely had more space in your parents' bathroom," he commented, kissing her cheek and neck. She made a mewling sound in her throat as she pressed her hand to his chest, pushing him to sit on the closed toilet. It took a few tries before she could properly unbuckle his belt, unzip his fly and pull out the part of him her body ached for. It took a few more awkward movements before she pulled down her slacks and sank on to him. She sighed with relief once she felt herself stretching to accept each glorious inch of his dick before she held his shoulders for balance and rode him. She rocked her hips back and forth before she raised herself up the length of him and then slammed herself back down. He traced his fingers up her spine in feathery motions before he started thrusting his hips up to meet her movements. They exploded together in jerky motions and loud cries that the plane's engine thankfully muffled. A bad bout of turbulence hit the plane before she'd even started coming down from her orgasm induced high and sent her barreling head first into Kofi. The *fasten seat belt* sign started flashing and she and Kofi began to laugh.

"Not a moment too soon," Kofi said as he helped her off him. They cleaned up and dressed as quickly as they could and Shae's heart beat hard against her chest until they were safely back in their seats.

"One of these days we will get caught," she warned Kofi as she settled back into the comfort of his arms.

"One of these days," he admitted with a wink. "But not today."

EPILOGUE

Shae adjusted the lighting again before stepping behind the camera to make sure she'd finally gotten it right. Kofi had asked her if she was ready for an adventure when they left Antigua and the adventure was greater than she'd bargained for. She'd travelled more, experienced more and loved more than she had in her entire life. Kofi had been right when he'd argued moving with him for the three months would be a great career move. Her new *A Caribbean Girl Takes London* series was her most popular to date. And then there was Kofi. Shae wasn't even sure how to describe the depth and color Kofi added to her life. Every day she woke up thinking there was no way she could fall more in love with him and then he'd say something, smile at her or do something so sweet and thoughtful that she could feel her heart melt. She was his and he was hers. Completely and irrevocably. Shae guessed that was why she felt it necessary to do what she was doing now. She glanced up at Kofi, who was sitting in the far corner of his office that he partially converted to a shooting room for her. He wore an orange shirt that looked sexy as hell against his deep brown skin. Couple that with his freshly trimmed beard and hair and Shae was barely avoiding jumping him. He was so damned gorgeous.

"Are you ready?" she asked.

"Lead the way."

One of the things that drew viewers to Shae's channel was her friendly, easygoing personality but despite that there were many things about her personal life she kept to herself. That was about to change. Kofi slid into a spot on the loveseat pushed against the wall as she started the camera. He pulled her into him and kissed her forehead when she sat back down.

"Let's do this."

The small, intimate move flustered her for a few seconds before she turned to the camera and smiled brightly.

"Hey guys, welcome back to my channel. I asked on Instagram and Twitter a few days ago to send in some questions because I was about to shoot a highly requested video. Welcome to my boyfriend tag."

She turned to Kofi. "Introduce yourself to the peeps."

He smiled into the camera and Shae couldn't stop herself from leaning closer to him. She almost felt sorry for the poor viewers who were about to be hit with the sexiness that was her man without warning.

"I'm Kofi," he said with that dimple showing smile. "And Shae has been in love with me for her entire life."

"Wow Kofi," she giggled. "That's really how you want to play it?"

"Just stating the facts, Shae Butter," he said, still smiling. He drew her into his arms and she suddenly forgot she was recording. "But I'm making up for lost time."

"Oh, really?"

"Yeah," he responded. His voice was soft now. "I love you so fucking much."

"I love you too."

She couldn't wipe the smile off her face so she took a while before she looked at the camera.

"I'll start with the most popular question," she said, turning back to Kofi. "How did we get together?"

His eyes sparkled and lips curved into that sexy smile when he said, "I was minding my damn business at this birthday party, right..."

THE END

AFTERWORD

I hope you enjoyed taking this journey with Kofi and Shae. They had a clear idea about where they wanted to end up and it was nothing like I first envisioned.

If you liked this book, please think about rating it and/or leaving a review on Amazon and/or Goodreads and telling your friends about it. Word of mouth is so important for indie authors.

Peace. Love. Light.
Rilzy

ABOUT THE AUTHOR

Rilzy Adams believes all you need is love. Or, at least it should. She may, or may not, be a huge Beatles fan. She spends too much time living in her head watching the romantic lives of her 'imaginary friends' play out and then being the chatty friend to tell the world about them. When she isn't living in her head, she must show up to work every day and be a lawyer. She resides, with her two dogs, on an island in the middle of the Caribbean Sea, which is perfect for her sun addiction, love affair with Prosecco and sushi worship.

For information on new releases, promotions and more: Join the Mailing List.

Visit her website at: www.rilzywrites.com

ALSO BY RILZY ADAMS

FALLING LIKE A JOHNSON SERIES

The Gift (Jaxon and Maya)
Will You Be Mine? (JT and Hallie)
Just One More Time (Orlando and Katrina)
When Love Ignites (Jasmine and Alec)
The Sweetest Escape (Jasper and Reign)
Yours Always (Orlando and Katrina)

UNEXPECTED LOVERS SERIES

Go Deep (Xander and Navaya)

LOVE ON THE ROCK BOOKS

Twelve Dates of Christmas (Zia and Rashad)
You, Me + Baby (Fran and Andre)
Brand New (Regina and Quentin)

SINGLES

Off Key (Zoe and Liam)
Love in the Time of Corona (Alyssa and Kingsley)

SHORT STORY COMPILATIONS

Love Bites – A Collection of Short Stories

Printed in Great Britain
by Amazon